"LOOK OUT! IT'S

The boom of shelling rattled the shielded warehouse, and Jack peeled open the seam of his armor, cursing Pepys all the while. Bogie crouched against his shoulder blade as he settled himself in the armor and seamed up. His wrists tingled, telling him his gauntlets were powered up and ready. As he bent to reach for his helmet, there was a screaming boom above, answered by a rending of metal, and smoke and fire poured in through the torn roof. He jammed on his helmet and looked up, even as the Talon's shadow began to dapple the skyline. Jack had target probability locked on before the strafing began again, and he fired his wrist rockets into the hellish miasma whirling overhead.

The shadow of the first Talon fled amidst flame and laser scoring, but the helmet tracking told him that two more attackers were approaching. He locked on to these new targets and raised his gauntlets, preparing to fire.

Metal screeched. Air exploded. A cascade of smoke and fire poured earthward. Jack had only a brief instant to realize the overhead roof, what was left of it, was coming down right on top of him. . . .

DAW Titles by Charles Ingrid

THE SAND WARS Series:

THE SAND WARS

RETURN FIRE
5

BOOK FIVE OF THE SAND WARS
CHARLES INGRID

DAW BOOKS, INC.
DONALD A. WOLLHEIM, PUBLISHER

1633 Broadway, New York, NY 10019

First Printing, August 1989

1 2 3 4 5 6 7 8 9

PRINTED IN THE U.S.A.

To Donald A. Wollheim,
the man who made science fiction possible. . . .

Prologue

Pepys, emperor of solar systems, sat in his communications web like a bloat-bellied spider, his frizzy red hair alive about a face furrowed in concentration and worry. His fingers twitched as his mind communed, but he found nothing he wanted in the data he combed.

He broke silence with a furious yell that echoed throughout the obsidite rose-pink hallways until his minister heard him and came running, security cameras panning every flap of his somber black robes as he answered the call.

Pepys was unplugging from his computer network when Baadluster gained the chamber. The emperor looked up, his pale, freckled complexion drawn in anger over the skeletal bones of his face. Vandover paused, thinking to himself that, underneath the anger, Pepys did not look well. An unwell emperor boded ill for the Triad Throne as well as for the Dominion, for Pepys was the war leader and main creditor of the armed forces. He was a brilliant man, but he had always reminded Baadluster of a small star shining brightly just before it went nova. The ambitious side of

Baadluster found the realization enlightening. He produced a smile.

"Can I help you, your majesty?"

Pepys pushed himself out of the chair holding his frail looking body. "Find him."

Baadluster lost his smile. Pepys' battle with the commander of the Dominion Knights was a war that had already drawn in and destroyed one ambitious successor to the throne. Baadluster might be found out and defeated, but he had no intention of fighting a losing battle not his own. He said cautiously, "Commander Storm was reported lost in the skirmish on Colinada. Although I give the Thrakian report as little credence as you do, your majesty, it appears the information is correct."

"And Saint Colin walked out of there unscathed while the best soldier in battle armor was blasted into ashes?" Pepys gave a snort of disgust.

"Then ask the Walker what happened. As a religious man, he should be predisposed toward lying."

"I have. He confirms the Thrakian story." Pepys shrugged into an over robe, its threads woven into a nearly impervious fabric. Its weight did not seem to tax the emperor's slight shoulders. The red-haired emperor had a wiry strength often overlooked. Pepys looked up, cat-green eyes glittering. "Jack is an idealist. I lost his trust when I made an alliance with the Thrakian League. In his eyes, we've sold out to our worst enemy. He understands diplomacy about as well as you understand the emotion of love. If you can't find him, find the girl. She'll find him."

"I know the whore has returned to Malthen. More than that—she doesn't carry an ID chip. She can go anywhere without being recorded." Baadluster shrugged. "He'll know she's being sought. He'll find another whore."

Pepys paused in the doorway of the chamber. He looked back, lips thinning. "Your assessment of Amber's relationship with Storm proves me out. The lady may be many things, but not a whore. I want Jack Storm found."

"Then just what do you suggest I do? I'm a Minister of War, not head of the World Police." The ambitious man who had lost his life trying to nail Commander Storm had been head of the security network. Baadluster had wasted no time in tapping into Winton's position, but it had all been unofficial. He spread his hands, large, flat appendages, in the air. "The Ash-farel keep me busy."

Scorn smoldered color back into the emperor's pale face. "Try the Green Shirts. He may have gone looking for the underground." Pepys drew up a corner of his robe, wrapped it nervously about one freckled hand, and smoothed it there. "He says he has full knowledge of who and what he was twenty-five years ago, but I doubt him. He's exhausted his options here—he'll have to go to them for answers."

Baadluster inclined his head, thick lips pursed in a noncommittal expression.

"And Vandover."

The minister looked up from the delicate, threadlike cable he had begun to roll up and put away. "Your majesty?"

"Spread the word that Storm is on an infiltration mission. If he reaches the Green Shirts, they won't trust him either."

"Yes, your majesty."

"I want him dead. If we can't find him and do it, perhaps they will."

Baadluster straightened. "Pepys—there appear to be two invincible forces operating in our space. The first is the Ash-farel, who are dangerous enough that they drove us to ally with the Thraks, and the second is Jack Storm. I respectfully remind you that opposing Commander Storm may not be wise. You've tried to take him out before. This time, he may feel free to return fire."

Fury filled the emperor to the point where he seemed to gain height. But he said nothing, turned heel, and left.

Baadluster found he'd been holding his breath. He looked at the fine cables draped over his fingers and dropped them on the communication chamber floor. Let the janitors clean up Pepys' messes. He followed after his emperor.

Chapter 1

Colin bowed his head and bent his shoulders. A dank wind blew thinning strands of hair across his brow, but it was not the element he cut his way against as he crossed the parking grounds toward home. Before he lifted his eyes to meet theirs, he could hear the clack of chiton and carapaces as Thraks shifted into a guard position, meeting him at his own door as though he were the enemy and not they. He met them squarely, the trio who had replaced his own long time bodyguard at the gated entrance to Walker headquarters, his rugged cross thumping upon his chest at his abrupt halt. He smoothed it down, aware the faceted eyes of the aliens accosting him watched every movement keenly, their expressions hidden behind kabuki masks of beetle armor.

The self-made minister to thousands swallowed a bitter taste in his mouth, reminding himself that they were no longer enemies, but allies. He no more believed it than he believed the lies of his long time friend Emperor Pepys, author of this misalliance.

"Identify yourself," said the Thraks to the

fore. Dark sable throat leather bulged with his implant.

Colin sighed. "Colin of the Blue Wheel," he said, disliking the way his voice sounded the moment the words were out. Old. Weak. Dispirited. He clenched his hand deep in the vest pocket of his overrobe. Had he traded all he'd once valued just to coexist?

The Thraks reached forward spindly fingers, crab claws with agility, bowing over him from its superior height. "Pass," it said.

The Walker saint thrust his jaw forward and moved between them forcibly though they had stepped aside to let him around them. With the clicking sounds of their alien flesh, they jostled each other to let him through, as averse to touching him as he was to touching them. Once inside his gates, burly Jonathan met him with warm hands, steadying him.

The ursinelike aide also topped him, but Jonathan exuded the milk of human kindness and, perversely, Colin felt smothered. He almost preferred the Thraks to this attention.

He snapped, "Leave me be."

"Your holiness . . ."

Colin came to a halt inside the foyer. He waited until the security doors slid shut and then said, "I'm sorry, Jonathan. You didn't deserve that."

The massive man's face closed in an expression that agreed with him. He moved to take Colin's outer vest, but the older man hugged it about himself, saying, "It's a little chilly. You can taste winter's edge out there—it may even rain later. I think I'll keep this on a while."

"I've got your apartment warming up. Shall I send up tea?"

Tea sounded good. "I'll take it up with me," he said. "I've the eulogy to work on. Tell Margaret to hold all my calls this evening." His aide nodded briskly and turned away to the kitchen

Alone at last, tea tray balanced in his hands, Colin mounted the steps to his private apartment. Audiences with Pepys were beginning to sap him, as though the emperor were a parasite of some sort, a devious being Colin must constantly spar with. Nor was Colin happy about being pressured into doing the eulogy for Commander Jack Storm, late of the Dominion Knights. There would be the inevitable military rites, all the more poignant because Jack was missing in action—his body had never been found. And, God willing, it never would be.

Taking the staircase an incline at a time, feeling his knees creak and watching the chinaware jiggle on the tray, steam puffing from under the teapot lid with each sway, Colin approached the only sanctuary he had left, a small but comfortable apartment hidden deep within Walker headquarters.

He set the tray down on the burled wood table from old home, long ago Terra, his knuckles brushing the polished surface. There was life in that touch, the life of wood still vibrant. With a sound half-sigh and half-groan, Colin lowered himself onto the comfort of his settee.

The room was deeply shadowed in late afternoon, but he did not call up his lights, preferring the comfort of dimness as he poured a cup and sat back, sipping the heated contents gingerly. The settee cushions embraced him.

"You're getting old," he muttered to himself. "Tolerating the enemy at your doorstep."

"I've never known you to tolerate anything," a shadow spoke back to him, and a man separated himself from the darkness of a corner.

Colin juggled his teacup, cursing as the hot liquid splashed on him. With a laugh, the tall man joined him and helped to blot up the disaster.

The minister sat back in exasperation. "Good God! What are you doing here—you're dead."

A sandy-colored eyebrow arched. "Rumors greatly exaggerated?"

"No, by God! I perjured myself, Storm, to give you a second chance. What are you doing here?"

Jack lowered himself into an expansive chair across from the couch. "I'm grateful for everything you've done."

"And we're both ruined if anyone saw you come in."

"I'd not be much of a Knight if I couldn't get past a few Thraks."

Colin's mouth twisted as he steadied his hands and reached for his teacup again. Pointedly, he did not offer his guest any. Storm did not need an invitation. He scooped up a cup with movement suggesting his long-fingered hands, one of them oddly missing the smallest finger, had handled much more delicate instruments. Colin had wondered for years how his friend had injured himself, but there were some questions one did not ask a free mercenary. And now, of course, Storm was no longer a mercenary, but a sworn

Knight, a fighting man mated to the technology of battle armor. But now Colin also knew, had learned, what had caused that injury, and others, which haunted the man. Being confined in cold sleep for seventeen years had taken its toll. Frostbite here, and other, more subtle and devastating changes elsewhere.

Jack waited for Colin to down half a cup. "What makes you so melancholy and testy this late in the day?"

St. Colin made a most unsaintly face. "I find myself faced with composing a eulogy."

"Ah." Storm added compassionately. "It happens to all of us, sooner or later."

"You should know," the man said dryly. "It's your funeral."

"What!"

"Don't tell me you didn't know. And here you are, making a liar out of me."

Storm put his teacup down, stood, and paced, the wood table an uncertain barrier between them. "It's only been a few months."

"The Thrakian ambassador has been pressing to take you off the MI list and have you officially laid to rest. Then he can press to have K'rok instated as permanent commander in your absence." Colin watched as Storm halted and several expressions flitted across the Knight's face.

"K'rok?"

"Who else?"

"I thought perhaps one of the Thraks—" he paused. "No. Milot or not, K'rok is probably the cagiest being for the job they want done, although

I don't know if the Thraks know what they've got a hold of—"

"They certainly didn't know with you," Colin interrupted. "But Milos has been under their claws for twenty-five years—"

Humor reflected in Storm's rainwater blue eyes. "Not long enough. K'rok was born free, and he grew up fighting Thraks. He only stopped to avoid extinction, and as soon as he finds a way to throw off their yoke, he'll do it. No, K'rok is as good a choice as any to head up the Knights. I think I'll stay dead."

Stress lines in Colin's face visibly relaxed as the prelate sank back among the cushions, teacup balanced on his knee. "I'm glad I was able to persuade you."

Storm paused in mid-stride, the irony not lost on him. He looked down. "I wouldn't have exposed you unnecessarily," he said.

"Thank you. *I* wouldn't have lied about you unnecessarily, but I seem to remember us coming to an agreement on that strategy. And, since we did, what the hell are you doing back on Malthen?"

"I think I've gotten you in enough trouble already." With a flexing of a young body still well in its prime, Jack sat. He did not reach for his teacup. "But I think I see an easier way of accomplishing what I need to. When's the funeral?"

"The day after tomorrow."

"You'll need a retinue?"

"Of course, I—" Colin plowed to a stop. He shook his head. "Oh, no. You're not sneaking in behind my robes."

"It's not for vanity. I need to get in. And I don't want to jeopardize Amber by contacting her."

"And do you honestly think, if I did bring you inside the palace grounds with me, that you'd escape *her* detection?"

Jack grinned. "I should hope not. But if she finds out, she'll play her part anyway. You know that."

"This . . . opportunity . . . you're looking for. It must be awfully important to risk coming back here."

Jack smiled thinly. "It is," he said. "It's my initiation into the Green Shirts."

The teacup bounced off the redwood table and shattered at Colin's feet. He did not seem to have noticed, all warmth fled from his face. "That's unconscionable. They're murdering scum, Jack—you're better off dealing with Pepys directly. He has to put on a public facade and that at least makes him maintain a veneer of civilization."

"They may be terrorists—but I haven't forgotten that they were the ones who found my cold ship and thawed me out."

"To make a pawn out of you," Colin pointed out.

"But they didn't succeed."

"Not yet anyway. It depends on what you've agreed to do for them. Destroy the Knights?"

Now Storm's weathered face paled slightly. "Never," he said, his answer clipped. "And you should know better than to ask."

"I do what I feel I must. I thought Pepys was your target . . . bringing down a corrupt administration is one thing, but replacing it with a terrorist organization is another. Every man has his price. I wonder what yours might be."

"They're giving me the name and location of the doctor who found me."

The two men looked sharply at one another. Then, softly, Colin asked, "Why? Why do you want to know after what they attempted to do to you?"

"Because he had to have kept records. The cold ship carried my looping—and I want that back. I want my goddamn memory back, intact, whole. I want my past. I want myself."

"That's a lot to ask," Colin murmured. "Are you sure it's what you truly want to face? There's a lot of us who would give anything to forget what happened yesterday and beyond." He cleared his throat. "And I hate that you must deal with scum."

Jack interrupted. "Odd. They speak very highly of you. I was given your name here on Malthen."

Colin surged to his feet with a strangled, "What?"

Before either man could say another word, the apartment com line signaled. Colin visibly gathered his wits, then answered, "What is it?"

The screen brought Jonathan into focus, but not before Storm deftly stepped out of viewing range. "I'm sorry to disturb you, but Denaro is here—"

Colin grabbed up his remote and thumbed on the mute. He looked at Storm. "He must know you're here."

Jack shook his head. Colin looked back to the monitor. "What seems to be the problem?"

Jonathan shrugged. He said confidentially, "He's armed to the teeth, your holiness. He seems to feel you might be at risk." He moved aside and the monitor camera panned a massive young man, dressed in trooper fatigues. Jack noted three weapons on his upper torso alone, not counting the cross hanging upon his chest which could be used in ways holy men had never intended.

"Tell him I'm in meditation and not to be disturbed."

Storm made a hand signal and Colin paused.

"He might be of use," Jack said.

"Not if he finds out you're in league with the Green Shirts."

The two men faced each other. Jack had trained Denaro to wear battle armor even though the militant Walker had ideas of his own about duty and honor and obedience.

"If you add me to your retinue, he'll have to know sooner or later."

Colin hesitated a moment longer but knew that if he had an honor guard escort of Walker priests, he'd also have a flanking pair of bodyguards assigned by Denaro and one of them would probably be the aggressive young man himself. "He won't be much use to you, Jack. Pepys has had him watched ever since he cashiered Denaro from the Knights."

"Then have him come back later. He won't be at ease until he sees you're all right."

That seemed appropriate. Colin nodded. He took the com off mute and said to Jonathan, "I've had a rough day. Give me an hour, and then I'll talk to Denaro, if he'll wait."

No answer was needed as the young man took up a chair in the corner of the lobby, staring intently through the monitor as if he could see into Colin's apartment. The com line hung up.

Jack said, "Denaro helped you cover for me."

"No question about that. He won't mind finding you here—but if he ever finds out you're associated in any way with the Green Shirts, your life is forfeit."

The sandy-haired man grimaced. "He'll have to stand in line behind Pepys and Baadluster and half a dozen others."

Colin took a step, heard the grinding of shards underfoot and looked down. He seemed to realize for the first time that he'd dropped his cup. With a dismayed cluck, he bent over and began to pick up the pieces, muttering, "Genuine porcelain."

"Does Denaro still have his armor?"

"No. Baadluster keeps an iron grip on the equipment. If there's any black market to be had, he probably runs it." Colin straightened, his attention still on the fragments in the palm of his hand. He stirred them. He looked up suddenly, with renewed fire in his brown eyes. "What do the Green Shirts say about me?"

"I was told to tell you I deal in artifacts, and that you might know a broker."

The fire quieted. "Ah. I do know a thief or two in that area. Did they intimate I was a Shirt?"

"No. And that I was to use discretion in inquiring." Jack tilted his head to one side, eyeing the Walker saint.

"And well you might, this or any other time." Colin cleared his throat in satisfaction. "I do not collude with the enemy!"

"You don't have to tell me that. But as to brokers...."

Colin closed his fist over the shards of porcelain he held. "Unfortunately, religious artifacts are bought and sold like any other commodity. Well, the best man I know is a real scoundrel in under-Malthen, a man named Gibbon."

Jack nodded in satisfaction, saying, "Then that's probably the man I need." He began to fade back into the long shadows from which he'd emerged.

Colin looked up abruptly. "Will you be buying or selling?"

"Selling," the man answered. "As soon as I steal two suits of armor."

"Your price of initiation. You know what the Shirts can do with weaponry like that."

"All I need to do is get in, make the contacts I need, and get out. I won't leave functional armor behind. You won't believe how difficult it is to man a suit unless you've been well-trained."

"I see."

"I hope you do. Talk to Denaro about me. I'll be back later. In the meantime, I'd like you to watch something for me." Jack had been blocking Colin's view of the shadowed far corner of the living room. Now something loomed beyond ... battle armor, in all its rugged and massive glory, its white Flexalink scales shining like nacre.

"In the name of God, man, you can't leave that here!" Colin fairly shook with agitation.

"I can't leave him anywhere else." Even as Storm spoke mildly, calmingly, the armor raised a gauntlet hand high as if in salute.

"Jack—God alone knows what kind of alien flesh is regenerating inside there, hooked up to your circuitry and power systems. Bogie's an embryo, a child, with the ability to destroy anyone and anything it doesn't comprehend—and not truly alive yet, how can it comprehend life?"

Jack let his right hand fall upon the Walker's shoulder. "I can't leave him alone. And because you know what he is—as much as anyone does— you know there's a soul there, as well as flesh. If anything happens to me, I'd like to know he's in good hands."

"Godfather to an abomination." Colin sucked in his breath. "Someday he could destroy you, Jack."

"Eat me up and spit the gristle out, like a Milot berserker? Maybe. But in the meantime, we have an understanding."

"You still wear your armor?"

Jack nodded. "He's all I've got. The little memory I have is from shared consciousness. And . . . we need each other. He's a warrior spirit, Colin, whatever else he is—and if that means that someday he has to turn on me in order to finish his regeneration, that's a chance I take. I think he'll give me warning."

"And then what . . . what will you do when he needs to feed?"

Jack gave a sinister smile. "Feed him Thraks."

Colin seemed to deflate under his hand. "All right," he said, "but only because he's too dangerous to leave untended."

"Thanks. I've some arrangements to make. But I'll be back later, and I'd like to know if I'm going as bodyguard or priest."

"All right," Colin agreed. Before his eyes, Jack seemed to fade from sight. The prelate listened, but could not really discern the Knight's manner of exit from his apartments, though the older man knew he should have been alert, for if Jack could get in or out, sooner or later someone else could. He looked down at his hand, and saw the shattered remains of his teacup still clenched within it.

He cupped both hands together and shook them lightly, the shards of his cup rattling about for a few seconds. When all was silent, he opened his hands, and smiled at the whole teacup resting within. Then a thought shadowed his pleasure, and his face. If only healing Storm could be that easy.

Chapter 2

"You'll go as a priest," Colin said. "Make that a reverend. Certain of the Walker sects are of monkish persuasion—you'll be in a hood and cowl. There's nothing very humble about your size—" the older man eyed Storm. "We'll put you next to Jonathan to shrink you somewhat. Denaro agrees with me, though. It's sheer folly to let you go and suicide to aid and abet."

"But you'll do it."

"Of course I will. What do you think I've been talking about?" Colin's speech lapsed as he lowered himself into his chair. For a moment, Jack perceived a flash of what the future would bring: the man grown older and feeble as the chair appeared to swallow him up, body hunched in weary surrender. But then Colin squared his shoulders and the future disappeared, his age apparent but not victorious as yet. He rubbed one hand across the knobby knuckles of the other in thought, then added, "We've only Amber to worry about."

"She knows I'm here."

"You told her?"

"Not directly—we both know that doesn't mean

she doesn't know. And why would you not want her to know?"

Colin opened his mouth as if to say something, thought better, and shut it. But the hesitation did not go past Jack. He stood over Colin. "Is there a problem?"

The prelate did not look up. He said quietly, "There's always a problem somewhere, if one looks hard enough. Pepys and Vandover deserve more consideration than you've given them."

Jack dropped into the chair opposite Colin. For a moment, it looked as if he would lean back and put his heels up on the priceless burled table, but instead, he leaned forward intently, upper body resting on his forearms braced by his knees. "Don't kid yourself. I've given the emperor *every* consideration. I haven't come this far to walk into his hands now. Or ever."

"I didn't mean—"

Storm waved his four-fingered hand. "I know, I know. But consider this ... with the Thraks infiltrating everything they can, at the behest of the alliance, Pepys is a dead man. Dead if the Thraks turn against him, dead if the Green Shirts can get their hands on him—dead if I expose him for the ambitious traitor he is."

Colin had not meant to flinch, meant even less that Storm should see it, but the clear blue gaze didn't miss much. He stopped, "I'm sorry, Colin."

"You've nothing to apologize for."

"I'd forgotten you and Pepys were close, once."

The older man scratched the corner of his temple, where his graying eyebrow had recently begun to sprout. The irony of it—fewer hairs on his head, more on his chest and in his brows—reminded him constantly of the contradictions of aging. He dropped his hand. "That was a long time ago," he said.

"And yet you're not surprised at what Pepys has done."

"Of course not. He's the emperor, isn't he? I've seen few emperors, or presidents, or even rebels for that matter, get where they are without walking over a lot of bodies. And you are very naive if you think otherwise."

"What about you?"

They considered each other, then Colin smiled gently. "Unfortunately," he murmured, "you'd find a sacrifice or two under my feet as well. But as few as I could possibly get away with—and no one who didn't know what they were doing."

Jack inclined his head. "Fair enough." He took a deep breath. "When do I get these reverend's robes?"

"Jonathan will bring them up. We've a few hours yet. Denaro will be in full equipment, in the honor guard. He says to tell you that he won't be using the dead man switch, whatever he means by that."

Jack considered the information with surprise that he quickly muffled. In answer to Colin's raised eyebrow, he said, "If there's trouble, and a man goes down, the armor is equipped to destruct if the man is pulled out before disarming the suit."

"What's he telling you, then? That he's not using the switch."

Jack nodded, saying, "In case of trouble. If he

goes down, if I can get to him, I can use the armor without worrying about disarmament."

They sat in easy silence for a moment, as if aware of the commitment made to each other, then Colin reached over the burled table, which felt to him like another living thing, and took Jack's hand. "I'll tell you now," he said, "for I may not have the time later. Once we leave these apartments, I'll not look at or talk to you. May God go with you."

Jack gave a sudden, lopsided and boyish grin, quite unlike the even baring of teeth in a battle smile which Colin had seen so many times. Colin had the eerie sense of seeing into Jack's very soul in that expression. "I hope He's quick—because once I get my hands on the armor I need, I'll be running like the very devil's on my heels."

Colin let out a short burst of laughter, then caught himself and quieted. "Denaro left this for you." He fished into a deep thigh pocket of his miner's pants and pulled out an address disk. "It's encoded with the current whereabouts of the fence you mentioned. He suggests that you visit him as soon as possible—the man's not going to be in business very long." He sighed. "I'm as naive as I've accused you of being. Pepys has to know of Gibbon's background—and I nearly hanged myself by associating with him. They found my weakness—both sides—and used it neatly."

"It's not your fault. That's what a Walker does . . . search for religious evidence."

Colin frowned. "We're more than that, much more. But you're right. It won't stop my looking. I shall simply be more circumspect about my contacts in the future. Be careful with Gibbon, Jack. You know the faction Denaro works with—fanatics are difficult to control. Denaro has left orders that will give the man time to deal with you and pass you on to the contacts within the Green Shirts—but whether he can exercise those orders or not. . . . Find Gibbon and make your contact. And hurry."

"I will." Jack's hand closed neatly about the address disk. Jonathan's heavy footsteps and large presence could be felt outside the apartment door. Storm smiled briefly. "Thank you. For everything."

Colin got up even as Jonathan rang for admittance. "Just," the older man warned, "don't criticize the eulogy."

Jonathan entered to laughter, and the great, burly man hesitated a moment, his gentle face frowning slightly as if he wondered if the laughter was directed at him.

A gray curtain of rain slanted across the parade grounds. It fell in spurts, wind-driven, a chill rain soaking the funeral procession. Far lightning struck. It illuminated the figures standing in the rain, and one of them lifted her head, turning slightly toward the electric glow.

She stood to the side, flanked protectively by taller figures, her face veiled from the cameras and audience, her thoughts her own. Thunder rumbled outside the city.

"It's almost over," the man at her elbow murmured. He was bareheaded, protected by the canopy overhead, a few wispy hairs of dark chestnut and gray ruffling across the top of his head, his strong jaw sagging a bit, but his eyes dark and full of challenge. He wore a dark blue overvest covering his plain miner's jumpsuit, various pockets flat and smooth for once. A simple cross hung against his chest and, unaware, he stroked it once before reaching for the slender young woman's hand. "It's almost over," he repeated.

She nodded. The veil shuddered with her movement. Then she said, "He would have liked the storm. Jack liked rain."

St. Colin did not respond except to tighten his fingers about her chill ones. Anything he might have said would have been drowned out by the military display coming to attention before them.

"Right, HARCH! Company, present!"

The ground trembled under the weight of battle armor. Faces obscured by their visors, the Dominion Knights filed past, their movements slow and somber, Flexalink shining dully in the overcast light. In a ripple, they began a salute to the woman in black and held it for their red and gold clad emperor as they passed the dais.

She did not turn toward Pepys as the armor passed, but he watched her. She knew it. She could feel the intenseness of his cat-green gaze upon the back of her neck and the slimy feel of that other's gaze—Baadluster. She leaned slightly toward Colin as if gaining strength from the man and repelled by the emperor and minister.

"Company, HALT! About face!"

The ground trembled one last time as the unit came about and stamped to a halt. Raindrops danced and glistened off the multicolored armor, massive and crude embodiments of the manpower it encased. Nowhere was there white armor—only one man she'd ever known had worn white. The veil across her face trembled. She could spot the few and scattered alien presences within the armor as well as those posted within the gates. Thraks, even here, even now. The corner of her mouth curled bitterly and she licked lips gone suddenly dry.

Colin loosened his hand from hers and stepped forward. The funeral began.

Vandover Baadluster stirred at his emperor's side. "She gives a very real performance," he commented, low-voiced.

Pepys sat up straighter within his voluminous red and gold imperial robes. The rain had taken the ever-present static from his red hair and it lay about him, restless, hovering, about to burst into its aureal state, but for the moment quelled. Not so the electricity of his cat-green eyes, and his stare flicked briefly from the presentation to his Minister of War's face, then back again. "Do I detect sympathy?"

"No"

"What then?"

Baadluster stood, his gaze fixed upon the military rite before them. His thick lips molded into a noncommittal expression as he ignored his emperor's jibe. "I am not sure," he answered finally, reluctantly.

"Good. You give her the flag. I have business elsewhere." Pepys gave a diffident wave of one hand. If he noticed the sudden tensing of the minister's body, or the clenching of his hands, he gave no indication, instead smothering a yawn as

St. Colin of the Blue Wheel began a eulogy. True to his word, as the funeral ended, he left his throne quickly, ostensibly to avoid a new curtain of rainfall slanting across the skies toward them, and Vandover found himself with the triangular folded company flag across his hands. He glanced at Amber.

She stood taller than he remembered, a distinctly regal aura about her slender figure, her face obscured by the dark veil. The fall of her tawny hair had escaped the veil and hung about her shoulders. She turned toward him expectantly.

He felt a jolt when their fingers touched as he transferred the flag to her palms. His chin jerked up, his gaze meeting the opaque veil searchingly— hadn't she felt it?

She closed graceful hands about the flag and said, "There are Thraks present, minister. They disgrace the armor. May I remind you it was the Thraks which killed Commander Storm?"

His nostrils flared. "This is not the time or place. . . ."

"No. Of course not. I forget that it was you who welcomed our enemies into our ranks." With a convulsive movement, the young woman hugged the flag to her chest. "He died so that we would all remember who our enemies are."

He leaned close. So close that he imagined he could clearly see her wide-set, expressive eyes— mellow brown heavily flecked with gold, amber, like her naming. "You mock the emperor, and you mock me. Storm is not dead. And I intend to find him."

Her words taunted him. "I hope you do, Baadluster. Hell isn't big enough for both of you. Perhaps Jack'll get sent home." She whirled on her heels and left him at the dais edge. The entourage of St. Colin's ministers closed ranks about her and followed.

Keenly aware that he was being watched by the troop and cameras, Baadluster drew himself up. He received the dismissing salute with dignity as well as hatred.

The sky rumbled, and rain began to fall in earnest. The video crew began to strike their equipment hastily, and, falling out, the troop broke into a jog leaving the parade grounds, their suits churning the area into waves of mud. Baadluster bowed himself against the elements and left swiftly. He did not notice that one of St. Colin's retinue splintered off.

Jack broke the lock code to the shops and stepped in quietly, looking around. No one from the dress troop would be in here yet, nor any of the support techs, for that matter. The locker rooms would be filled to the brim as they stripped the muddy suits and sluiced them down before loading the equipment racks. He had time to do what he'd come for.

The sight and smell of the shop rooms gave him pause. Memories flooded him of all the time he'd spent in shops like this, stripping down, cleaning, and repairing his armor. In makeshift tents on frontier Milos, in the mercenary shops side by side with his friend Kavin, now dead. Even here on Malthen where he'd sworn false allegiance to a false emperor. He felt no guilt for what he did now because the loyalty he'd sworn was only valid if the ruler also upheld his oath.

Jack stirred. The security systems would be picking him up soon, whether he wore the white light shield clipped to his belt or not. Besides, he did not have the faith in electronic gadgetry that Amber had. He swiftly located the inspection and racking area and found what he needed.

New suits, never worn, one still lying in its packing crate. Jack deftly resealed it and found a crate for the second, then loaded them on the power sled for transportation. He coded them for delivery to a blind address, where help he'd hired would redirect them, making tracing difficult if not virtually impossible. He jimmied open the dock doors and watched the power sled disappear into the darkening afternoon. He should follow them out, but the loading docks were strictly automated and his body heat would set off alarms and consequences he'd be better off avoiding. He sealed the double doors shut again and, passing through one of the diagnostic rooms, paused, then pocketed one of the new probes racked there, thinking Bogie could use some fine tuning.

He had almost made it back to the entry when a voice stopped him in his tracks.

"I just headed up a memorial service for you, commander. I didn't believe the rumors."

Hair prickled on the back of Jack's neck. He'd half-expected to meet someone in the shops—he'd hoped they'd be Thraks or Sergeant Lassaday. Thraks he'd kill cheerfully and Lassaday, with a bit of explanation and persuasion, could be expected to let his commander pass.

But the voice was young, strong, and clear—and he turned to face a man who was everything Jack might have been, had he not been betrayed. Rawlins stood in a corridor entrance, the dim light shining off hair that was silver-blond, eyes the intense blue of bottomless pools watching him in accusation, whole and unscarred of limb and soul. Jack was a soiled mirror-image of the young man, his own hair muddied, his blue eyes lightened, grayed by truth rather than innocence, he liked to think. He'd always found it difficult to face Rawlins, and this meeting was no less painful.

"Rawlins. Seeing ghosts?"

"Sir." The officer shifted weight easily, then said, "It is you. I thought so, but I hoped—from the back—I could have been mistaken."

Jack studied the distance between them, gauging not only how quickly he could get to Rawlins, but to see if the blanking shield would cover them both. His calculation was uncertain. In any case, he could not afford to stand here and attempt to repair the damage done to Rawlins' idealism. "I'm going out the door, Rawlins, and you will not have seen or talked to me."

"Is that an order, sir?"

Jack shook his head. "No. A request, one that will benefit you perhaps even more than it will me."

The jawline tightened. Rawlins looked pale in the twilight illumination. His eyes glittered. "Then it's true. You've gone AWOL."

"Nothing is ever exactly as it seems." He took a half-step back, toward the door.

Reflexively, Rawlins' hand went toward the weapon he carried. Jack stopped.

"Tell me what is true, then."

Jack shook his head even before the other's words finished ringing in the corridor. He half-raised his open, weaponless right hand, the four-fingered hand scarred by cold sleep. "There isn't time, and it's better you don't know."

"Is it the Thraks?"

Jack didn't answer, unwilling to lie, even partially. His defection was in part due to the Thrakian alliance, but there was so much more.

"Nothing is that uncomplicated," he told the former aide. He searched his memory of Rawlins and found a way out. "One of these days, when you have time, and you think you can handle the consequences of knowing the truth . . . you might discuss it with St. Colin."

Rawlins' face blanched. Jack was unsure of what he'd touched off there, knowing only that his aide had had ties with the Walker reverend during their campaign on Bythia. Rawlins would believe what Saint Colin deigned to reveal, and Jack knew he could trust Colin to be discreet. Jack took another stride backward, hand still upheld.

"There isn't time," he said, "to tell you more."

Abruptly, Rawlins nodded. His posture changed to one of defeat, his chin dropped. Then he looked up.

"Take me with you."

"You can't go where I'm going. You're still a

Knight." Jack's voice sharpened, a whip crack across the space between them. "Sometimes the hardest enemy to fight is the one that walks shoulder to shoulder with you. We all do what we have to do, lieutenant."

"Captain," corrected Rawlins softly, but he gathered himself. "Yes, sir. Thank you, sir." He turned heel and left.

"No," Jack added softly to the emptiness. "Thank you." He found the door and escaped.

Chapter 3

"He got in all right?" Colin paced before Denaro, not looking at the captain of his private army, but well aware of the heavily armed and armored man taking up the majority of room in his apartment.

"No one followed him, your holiness," Denaro said. "I could not observe without attracting attention."

The Walker prelate ignored the disapproval flavoring Denaro's words. He had already been through this argument with the young warrior, and he'd already made his position clear. Storm was to be given whatever aid he needed. Discreetly if possible, openly if necessary. "Good. Then he'll be making contact with Gibbon this evening. Pass the word. Gibbon's offices are to be kept clear until Storm's done his business. Then, and not before, you can shut him down."

There was a slight hesitation before Denaro answered in the affirmative. Colin met his gaze. He said nothing, but he knew that he was faced with a man who might have plans of his own in the working. If so, there was nothing he could do about it now. To vent his suspicions now might be extremely foolhardy—and destroy what confidence Denaro had in his leadership. To wait might lead Jack into a trap—but Colin could not avoid that, no matter how he wished. Trust was all. He looked into Denaro's deep black gaze.

"Good. Then all we have to do is wait. If all goes well, Jack will be back before he goes off planet."

Denaro burst out, "That's stupidity. He'll risk incriminating you."

Colin scratched a bushy eyebrow. "Maybe," he answered slowly. "But I have something he wants and needs very badly." He looked over Denaro's shoulders to the hulk of white armor waiting silently and sullenly in a corner as if it were a living, thinking thing.

Which, in many respects, it was.

Colin sat down, crossed his legs, and picked up his meditation studies. He looked up briefly at Denaro. "Relax," he advised. "It's going to be a long night."

Jack took almost as many blind routes as the suits did before he gathered up the power sled, transferred the two large crates to yet another power sled, and keyed in the address to Gibbon's disreputable offices. Nightfall had curtained even this section of under-Malthen which was now garished with neons and a never ending stream of humanity looking for and fulfilling vices in a variety of ways.

Gibbon was a quiet, hardworking businessman. The neighborhood he'd chosen to do business in was the same. Jack approached the loading dock in the rear cautiously, scanning the building's eaves for security systems panning the vista.

He saw none, but that didn't mean he wasn't being observed. He put the power sled on idle and knocked on the door.

A synthetic voice droned out of the speaker. "We're closed."

Jack was in no mood for argument. He looked at the silver mesh which hid the source of the voice. "Green Shirt" was all he answered.

The door snapped open immediately, and then the loading dock slide as well. Jack put the sled on auto and stepped through the doorway.

Gibbon was a massive slab of a man, head sunk into a pair of shoulders that seemed as wide as the loading dock doors. His eyes glittered as he looked Jack over. Jack caught the bloodshot glow of greed in them.

His right ear was a rack of jewelry that chimed softly as he looked toward the crates being delivered into his storeroom, and then back toward Jack.

"I may or may not have been expecting you," the man said. "But some things are damned stupid talking about on the street." He opened a beefy hand and waved Jack into the depths of the store.

Jack looked about the scatter of crates and shipping cartons, dim corners and far recesses. Under his heel, he heard the echo of a false floor, and smiled thinly. "Some things are damned stupid doing," and he shook off his host's invitation.

Gibbon's thick hand clenched. The jewelry

quivered noisily, and his eyes boiled with anger. "Are you here to do business with me or not?"

"I thought you were closed."

"I thought you were someone else." Gibbon swallowed convulsively.

"I might be yet," Jack said. "Or you might be."

"Ah! Is that the reason for your shyness? Well." The shopkeeper's closed expression opened up, and he gave a sardonic laugh. "Good enough. What shall I do to identify myself, for it's obvious you don't know anyone who knows me. I'm not the sort of man easily forgotten or duplicated." He threw his arms out and did a pirouette, in the graceful way the very large sometimes have, as though it were the sun and moon that orbited around them instead of the other way.

Jack felt a moment of guilt that this man would cease to exist shortly after doing business with him. He offered his hand. "Call me Jack," he said.

"I will. And you may call me Gibbon. And who sent you to me?"

"Saint Colin of the Blue Wheel."

"Ah! Aha! That confirms it. And these two lovely cartons contain my shipment."

"No."

Gibbon had turned and was making his way to the office portion of his warehouse, a room Jack could barely glimpse through a privacy curtain, a room no less cluttered than the docks. He came to an abrupt stop.

Jack gave an apologetic shrug. "There is a matter of payment. . . ."

"Ah." Gibbon nodded heavily. "Of course. *Then* it becomes my shipment."

Jack smiled.

From inside the cuff of his sleeve, Gibbon produced several short plastisheets. Jack caught the flash of a surgery scar, across the wrist flesh where ID chips were usually implanted, and was in the process of reaching for the plastisheets when they, and Gibbon's hand, disappeared in a laser flash.

Jack cried out and hit the floor, and began to crawl backward toward the dock gridway. Gibbon grabbed his stump of a hand with a bloodcurdling scream and did a dance upon his false-bottomed floor. It rolled under his bulk with the sound of thunder.

The lights went off, replaced by an orange gleam. He could still see Gibbon's vast body in a black silhouette ballet as a second bolt caught the man in the chest, yellow-white, lighting up the storeroom for a moment. Then the false flooring gave way under Gibbon's weight, and the man disappeared from view with a crash.

Jack heard the shouts and cries of disappointment as men filled the storeroom.

A half-melted, charred piece of plastisheet kited across the floor and under Jack's hand as he backed farther into the loading dock. Convulsively, he picked it up and shoved it inside his jacket. The Green Shirts had promised him considerable payment for delivery of the suits: credit, IDs, maps leading him to further contact. He had no time to see what minor scrap of the payment had survived.

A hand reached out and prevented him from moving.

"Give it a minute," the soft voice whispered in his ear. "I can guarantee Gibbon will come up firing. When he does—we're out of here."

The voice he would know anywhere, the owner he would trust with his life. Jack felt his face crease as he gave a genuine smile into the twilight.

"I told Colin you'd know I was back."

"Damn right," Amber said. "And you're in trouble as usual." But she didn't sound angry with him.

Amber graced the sofa of the saint of the Blue Wheel, her slim form reclining across the furniture as though she didn't have a bone in her body. The pose was a sham and both Colin and Jack knew it. She radiated nervous energy the way the Malthen sun radiated heat, and she watched both men as they talked quietly.

Colin ran his hands through his thinning hair one more time. "I feared Denaro might pull something like that. It was unforgivable of me to send Amber after you ... and to think he could be trusted."

"Don't apologize for him. I'm out of it. They left the shop burning, and for all he knows, I burned with it."

"Which you would have," Amber pointed out, "except Colin's tongue would snap off before he could tell a lie. I know that section of town. You had no business going in there without me."

The two looked at one another across the room,

various passions revealing themselves on Amber's expressive face.

"I know," Jack answered softly. "But I also know the emperor's probably watching you. I didn't want to make things more difficult."

"Difficult was leaving you six months ago so you could play dead. Hell is living as though you are dead." Amber looked away suddenly, as if she'd said too much.

The Walker cleared his throat and muttered, "Damn the boy, anyway."

Jack's clear blue eyes pinned Colin momentarily. "He could have been protecting you."

Colin blinked. "Or had motives of his own. I'm not forgetting the militarist faction among my followers. You've got to get off Malthen as soon as you can. I can't shield you any longer. He'll know once he sees the armor missing anyway. He'll know you survived and took it with you."

At the mention of armor, Jack's gaze veered off to where it stood. He said, "I can't leave Bogie behind."

"Then I'll have to learn how to control Denaro." Colin paused, and examined the plastisheet Jack had given him. "And to answer your second question, yes, I have the resources to reconstruct this, but you don't have the time. What is this, anyway?"

"It's my payment for turning the battle armor over. I requested some information and was also promised a lead to joining with the Green Shirts officially."

Colin frowned. "You know my feelings on that."

"And mine as well. But I can't bring Pepys down without them, and we need to know as much about the organization as we can ... or we'll just have replaced one evil with another."

"Then you'll have to act on what can be read. Do you know who you're looking for?"

Jack gave a bittersweet smile. "Oh, yes. This is the man who brought me out of seventeen years of cold sleep."

Amber sucked in her breath. "He won't want to see you coming."

"I know. That's one reason we're taking Bogie with us."

Chapter 4

A dirty night rain had pelted the streets and concrete lots of under-Malthen, washing away a thin veneer of misery. It left behind a sheen of grit and oil that muffled sight as well as sound, embracing stealth which was well for the denizens of under-Malthen, to whom crime was like air.

The three unlikely figures hid in the shadows outside Mentech's security doors. Slim and lithe, the first, in dark colors and hooded, worked intently at the computer alarm system. She had breached the conventional security system and seemed unaware of the camera she had not detected, or the vision it relayed. The second, a tall, big-shouldered man who took no pains to conceal either his plain, strong-featured face or sandy hair, bent over the figure clothed in black. The last, shadowing the pair, was a massive thing, white armored, opalescent in the thinning light of the moon. A robot, perhaps, or a cyborg, though from its size and armory, it was not a civilian machine. That thing had been built to win wars.

All three made an impact on the two men

watching them through the monitor's hidden screen.

The tall man made an impatient gesture. "Why can't we hear them?" The sleeve of his plastic lab jacket flopped extravagantly about his thin, bony wrist.

"They've got a white sound barrier up."

"How did they get so close before the monitors picked them up?"

The gray-haired little man in a uniform of gray as dull as his hair color hunched into himself. "I don't know, doctor. Professionals. I would suggest the one in the fore is a thief. . . ."

"We have nothing worth stealing here!" The doctor held his arms folded defensively across his chest, one hand free to rub the side of his large, thin nose. That was not strictly true but he had no intention of letting his security personnel know of the wealth as well as the experiments protected inside the lab buildings. He sucked in his breath. There was no time to waste: his operation had been made and whether the trespassers were illegal or enforcers made little difference. He had no idea who they were or what they wanted—but they triggered his decision. He decided to cut his losses. It had had to happen one day. Today was as good as any.

"Hold the door," the doctor said. "As long as you can." He walked away, leaving his employee nervously watching the one monitor the thief had not decommissioned. His voice drifted down the hallway. "There'll be a bonus in it for you."

The doctor's mistake. At that promise, the gray-suited man told himself he would not lay down his life for his employer—otherwise, how could he collect a bonus? But he would do everything else in his power. He keyed open the storage yards for the android intruder force.

Five doors slid open. Five pewter colored machines glided out. Servos whined smoothly, joints flexed, weapons charged. The security patrolman fed in the images of their targets, his fingers flying over the keyboard. Then he sat back to watch his job being done.

The doctor took the first corridor hover he could find. He keyed on his belt com. After a slight crackle, a hoarsely feminine voice said, "What?"

"We've been made. Shut the labs down and burn them. Start with 1, 3, and 4. I'll be taking care of 2 personally."

"What?" Her amazement crackled over the line.

"There's no time, dammit! Do what I said. All that matters is that the two of us and our records get clear."

"Right. Labs 1, 3, and 4. I'll meet you in 2—"

"No. Outside the buildings, in the back lot."

The voice quavered a bit, then said, "It's that bad?"

"Yes."

"We can't fight for it?"

"No! Stop arguing."

Her voice, tinged with loathing, protested, "Jeez, I hate that tunnel. All right. Be careful."

The doctor paused a moment before squeezing off the com button. "You, too," he said faintly, his voice off the air. He leaned with the hover as it turned a sharp corner.

Amber said irritably as the massive piece of battle gear shuffled his boots impatiently for about the twentieth time, "Three more connections and we're in. Just hold on."

"Onto what?" the armored structure said, his voice deep and resonant, a being of operatic tones inside a personified tank.

"It's a figure of speech." Jack spoke as if instructing a young child. "Be quiet so Amber can concentrate." He stood closest to the woman and could feel the tension generating in every fiber of her being as she cupped the alarm system. It did not help that she knew he would be leaving as soon as he got what he wanted, that he would not allow her to continue on with them. She had argued long and loud her value to him, and her presence here and now confirmed the fact that he needed her skills.

She had her mane of dark honey-colored hair tucked away inside that skintight hood, but he could still smell the fragrance she used as he leaned close. It made his thoughts wander. . . .

"Give me room," she whispered. "One wrong connection and we'll have sweepers all over us. I don't need the police—and you're supposed to be dead."

He stood back slightly.

"Not," she added out of the side of her mouth, "to mention that a lot of people have gone to a lot of trouble—"

"I know" he interrupted her mildly.

As if she read his thoughts, as indeed she might have, Amber said, "It's worth it, if we can break the Thrakian alliance and Pepys."

"It's a web," he answered. "The way they've tangled themselves up in everything, it'll take a lot of unweaving. A lot of strand-breaking."

She repeated. "Worth it." She hunched over a moment and made a slight noise in her concentration. The sound deflector on her belt continued its pulsation.

The armor at his back brushed his shoulder with a gauntlet and left it resting there. He patted the gauntlet. "Soon, Bogie." The alien used the battle gear casually as an eggshell. Jack both befriended and feared that entity, a situation as close to fatherhood as he'd ever gotten.

"Got it." She straightened up and saw him watching her. "Ready?"

"As we'll ever be. Now remember, the grounds are massive. I want Dr. Duryea, no one else."

Bogie rumbled. "Use stun?"

"Yes."

There was an echo of disappointment from the armor. Childlike though he was, Bogie had the blood lust of a Milot sand berserker. Amber smiled faintly, the lines of tension erased from about her gold-flecked brown eyes. Jack passed her the palm laser he'd been holding. He had his own weapons, gauntlets to the wrist not unlike Bogie's firing power, gauntlets scavenged from another suit of armor, and stripped down. His pants hid the power lines running to his Enduro bracer-armored calves and boots, power supplies jury-rigged there. Amber's slight frown returned as she looked down.

"One misstep and you'll blow your own foot off."

"Never. I know what I'm doing." Actually, she was quite possibly right. He had done his own jury-rigging. Although a soldier knew his armor intimately—it was, after all, his life—a soldier didn't have to be an engineer to wear one.

"Open sesame," Amber said mockingly, reaching around and slapping her hand on the lock. "What are you going to say to the good doctor when he finds out we've broken in."

Jack grinned fiercely. "Thank you."

There are times when every soldier expects to see his life pass before his eyes. Transport ships from military zones and engagements routinely use a debriefing loop to extract information and de-stress troopers during cold sleep. It was routine—nothing should have gone wrong. But it had.

It had started with the Thrakian invasion of Milos, an invasion which the Dominion forces could have turned aside. Would have turned aside if they had not been betrayed and cut off. Storm had been one of the few men left alive to make it to a transport. And then, that ship had been damaged during lift-off and gone adrift, lost.

Lost for seventeen years. Faced with his memories of a disastrous military engagement for seventeen years. Memories that burned out the deeper recall of his youth and his family, now dead by Thrakian hands.

Now he was about to face the man reported to

have found him, sole survivor on a burned out hulk of a transport ship, and thawed him out.

"Thank you" was only one of the things he meant to say.

Mentech's access door snailed ajar, releasing a draft into the night air that smelled of disinfectant and other, more foreign, less identifiable scents. Bogie lumbered forward with an impatient growl and ripped the door off its track. His gauntlets crumpled the plating as if they were plastisheets.

Dismayed, Jack caught a glimpse from the corner of his eye down the right corridor, reached out and slapped Amber down even as he yelled, "Take it off stun, Bogie! Take it off stun!"

All hell broke loose as the intruder force opened fire. Jack felt Amber under his shoulder as he elbowed himself up. Laser spray passed over him, a hot curtain, sparks floating down from the metal and plastic framework it seared. He cocked his gauntlet. Power tingled along his bare wrists inside the armament. Without coming up off the floor, he fired back.

Bogie had caught one of the robot force dead center. Its smoking ruins had come to a halt in the corridor lobby, half-melted, its pincer arms at spindly half-mast. Even destroyed, it looked deadly.

The other four moved so fast Jack couldn't track a target. Under his shoulder, Amber made a muffled noise.

"When I roll," Jack told her, "run for it."

She made a noise like a spitting cat. "Damned

cheap contraband," she added. "My gun shattered when we hit the floor."

He couldn't let her go unarmed. If even one of the sentries got past Bogie and him, it would track her down through the streets. "I'm going to the right," he said then.

"I'll shadow you."

A silver spider whirled past him. Jack kicked out in reflex, knocking its weapon out of alignment and the plasma blast intended to dispose of them instead ripped what was left of the door out of the framing. He got to his knees and felt Amber skittering past behind him. He fired once, aimlessly, to cover her.

Mentech's lobby was all business; ten paces across he spied double doors with palm locks and a face plate that probably read retinal patterns. Bogie's handiwork left an unusual sculpture in the center of the room. To the right was the wall, and to the left a corridor that disappeared around the corner—a corridor that undoubtedly led to a storage room where the intruder force had been stored. Jack now had his back protected by a corner.

Bogie knew where they were, had tracked them the moment they moved, and did not fire their direction. He pivoted to his left and his gauntlets burst in rapid fire. A second robot exploded in sparks and smoke. Jack flinched away from the eye-burning sight even as Amber grabbed his shoulder and screamed.

His hand came up in reflex, pointed, and squeezed. They were showered by metal and smoldering plastic fragments and he realized the thing must have been overhead.

Through the smoke, he could see two more pewter objects bent toward them, skirting Bogie. Why didn't the armor draw them?

He must have muttered aloud, because Amber's voice hoarsely answered, "Heat! They have to be heat sensored."

And Bogie was cold. The only heat he possessed was his weapon fire.

Jack sighted and fired at a five-armed beauty only a mechanic could love. It staggered, rocked back on its tread, then came on again.

Bogie snagged the last machine and, awash in its laser fire and impervious to the weaponry, began to take it apart.

Jack and Amber bolted to their left. He went down on one knee, skidding, felt his jury-rigged wiring pop—he hoped it was his wiring—and fired a second shot even as the wall opened up in flame where they'd just been. His left gauntlet went dead, his wrist ice-cold.

A tensor arm shattered. The robot skewed around, bringing its undamaged arms and turrets into play.

"Shit," Amber said, and he heard a noise at his heels that sounded like she'd flattened full out on the floor.

Bogie literally had his hands full. Jack eyed the machinery coming at them, well-oiled, smooth, deadly, and targeting them.

He picked its locomotion out and fired. The robot ground to a halt, its base shattered. But from the turets and muzzles facing them, Jack had no doubt he was well within range.

"Run!"

"No," said Amber, muffled. "Just quit playing around and frag that son of a bitch!"

He laid down a spray across its chest, even as he dodged to his left, his knee giving out completely. A muzzle melted. Laser fire limned the wall where his chin had been. He felt it like a close shave and fired back.

He missed, but it drew Bogie's attention. The white armored being paused, hands in the air, the netlike remnants of a robot hung between his fingers.

Amber reached up, grabbed Jack by the throat, and jerked him down even as their sentry fired. He felt the heat sear across the back of his head.

"Close," the girl muttered, "but you're not bald yet."

They lay in an entangled embrace. Jack hugged her close as servos whined and they were targeted once again.

Bogie fired. The robot paused, as though absorbing the energy. Then, abruptly, it shattered.

In his arms, Amber let out a ragged breath. Her warm, dry lips brushed his cheekbone before she said, "I think they know we're here."

Jack got to his feet and pulled her up. He bent over to examine his left bracer. The wires had been severed—his left hand firepower was out for the night. He'd have to make do with the dwindling charge in his right glove.

"What are the odds they have more of those babies around the corner?"

Amber shook her head, and trembled within his loose embrace. Bogie kicked over a tarnished hulk and crunched his way toward them. "Which way, Boss?"

Jack looked over Amber's shoulder toward the double doors.

Amber leaned against the computer clipboard in the wall next to the hand lock and examined it critically. Her nose wrinkled slightly across its bridge. "Your doctor's been a bad boy," she said, as Jack looked into the small, sealed lab, the third of its type they'd come across.

"Find the access code?" he asked, without turning his attention away. The gleaming counters, the suit-waldos waiting to penetrate an entrance from the side walls, the incubators full of petri dishes ... research interrupted. Bogie leaned a shoulder against the sealed door. Jack felt his ears pop as the suit interfered with the presurization. He touched the Flexa linked elbow. "Leave it," he said, and turned his attention to Amber. "Are you in?"

"I'm in, and the news isn't good. You don't want in there—or anywhere. Dr. Duryea is a genetic engineer, and an illegal one, if these notes are right." She shuddered. "We're going to end up with something real nasty if we break those seals."

"No kidding." Jack took up a stance behind her, reading the computer clipboard.

"Uh-oh." There was a line break across the flow of information. Amber dropped a hand to his wrist. "These labs are rigged to blow."

"What?"

"Somebody's set them in destruction sequence." She turned off the computer. "At least these babies aren't getting out of here alive."

"How long have we got?"

"Seven minutes."

Jack stepped back into the corridor. He made a sweep. "Bogie, take that T-intersection. Stun for the doctor, full power for anything else."

The opalescent armor turned and went the way he'd indicated. Amber watched critically. "Sure that was a wise thing to do? His judgment is a long way from being developed."

"No worse than yours, guttersnipe," Jack returned.

She made a face at him, an expression that belied the handsome young woman she'd grown into and reminded him of the panhandling youngster he'd first met years ago. "Then I'm going with you. If this is an indication of what Mentech is up to, we're likely to meet something nasty and full-grown just around the corridor."

As they jogged, his gauntlet up and ready for anything that might cross their path, he said, "What was the firing sequence?"

"This wing from front to back lot, and the wing Bogie took."

"That's it?"

"There's another wing, an L section." Amber considered and jabbed a thumb in the approximate direction. "According to the schematic, that's not been given the sequence yet."

Jack smiled. "Then that's the way we go."

She gave him a chill look. "Maybe," she said, "fire won't kill what's in those labs."

He pretended he hadn't heard her.

Duryea paused at the hydra's tank. He ran a gloved hand fondly over the molded lip of the container. There was a stirring within. "Sorry," he whispered. "Another job incomplete. But your owner will be just as delighted with my research report. Cheaper, but still conclusive." He reached up and turned off the respirator pump guarding the inflow to the covered tank. There was nothing for a moment, then the liquid within began to froth furiously. Eventually, lavender blood tinged the foam. Duryea watched as the roiling liquid slowly calmed. He heard a muffled explosion and knew the destruction sequence had begun in Wing 1. He popped a chip out of the wall clipboard and slipped it in his pocket.

The sealed doors behind him opened and he said, without turning around, "I thought I told you to wait beyond the tunnel—"

"Sorry, doctor. You didn't leave instructions at the door."

Duryea whirled and saw the tall man and the thief blocking the doorway. In the muted laboratory light, he identified the thief now as a woman—and a nicely curved one, beneath the black cloaking. "Everything's destroyed," he said. "There'll be no evidence."

"We hardly look like sweepers," the young woman answered, her voice heavy with irony. "Now, do we?"

"It matters little." The palm laser hanging in

the depths of his right lab pocket seemed to shift of its own accord. Duryea casually began moving his hand downward. "You've seen what I do here. I scarcely want police attention any more than you do. Who are you?"

The tall man shifted. He tilted his head back slightly, and the doctor got the full impact of his clear blue gaze, eyes the color of lake water on a good day. He knew those eyes. . . .

The flicker of recognition had been seen by the other. He smiled ever so slightly. "You do know me, doctor."

"What are you doing breaking into my labs?"

The man took a step closer. He wore massive, armored boots and gauntlets, and there was the stink of laser fire about them. The doctor shrank back instinctively against the hydra's tank, knowing them for weapons. "I just came to say thank you, but you're a suspicious man. All this research, up in smoke."

"Thank you?" Duryea kept sliding his hand lower, dipping it closer to his pocket. The man was his target, the young woman appeared unarmed. A clean shot to the throat, and he was out of there, before his lab joined the destruct sequence.

"Yes. You found a transport drifting out of range." That rainwater gaze looked about briefly, appraising the lab. "I suppose I should be grateful all you did was revive me. I could have been spliced into something more . . . unusual."

Duryea felt his heart convulse in his chest. He grabbed for his laser, but the other outdrew him, and he found himself on the floor, in a puddle of hot, wet substance. It was difficult to breathe.

"Storm. . . ." the doctor got out.

The named man went down on one knee beside him. "What the hell did you do that for," he said angrily. "I didn't come here to kill you!" He frowned as he searched Duryea for other weapons, and his palm skidded on fabric growing steadily bloodier. "You haven't got long. Who pulled me out and why? Why wasn't I reported to the Dominion as a troop survivor?"

Duryea felt his throat fill with fluid. He gargled and spat, so that he could speak. "We're all weapons in the war—" he said.

"Green Shirt?"

Words failed. The doctor found the strength to nod. Yes! For all his sins, he'd done something right. He'd been a member of the revolutionary Green Shirts.

"And you hid me."

The doctor nodded again.

"I was a Dominion Knight!"

Duryea's right hand began to quiver convulsively. It danced among the blood and gore upon the flooring. "Pepys ... had the Knights destroyed. You, too, if. . . ."

"What about my *mind*? Where's the tape of my debriefing loop? Was it taken off the transport? Who's got my artifacts?"

Duryea's chin met his chest. It was sticky and smelled like burning meat. The doctor felt his thoughts become dizzy and spin off, one by one. He got out, "The Countess has it . . ."

"Who?"

"The Countess," the doctor repeated. "Find her, find yourself." He coughed, and there was no breathing through that gargle. He followed his last thought into darkness.

"Jack," Amber said tightly. "We've got about ninety seconds to get out of here." The display light from the lab's wall clipboard illuminated her face with a ghastly glow.

He stood. His boots glistened with the doctor's blood. He keyed on his belt com. "Bogie—get out of here *now*!"

He took Amber's hand.

"Be careful what you ask for," she said faintly. She put a boot toe in the doctor's rib cage and nudged gently. "You just may get it. Has it occurred to you that if he couldn't alter you directly, he may have edited the looping tape?"

Jack took her by the elbow and led her outside. He left the door open.

"That's a chance I'll have to take, isn't it?" Jack listened to the explosions, growing louder, more destructive.

"Suppose you remember a long lost lover?"

He looked down then, and met her gold-flecked eyes. "Then I guess she'll just have to stay lost," he said softly. "For the night, anyway."

Amber smiled and slipped her hood back, loosening her hair. The hall drummed with the sound of battle armor running toward them. She sighed. "I don't suppose there's a way to turn him off for the evening?"

"He'll never notice," Jack answered. "He's more interested in the vidscreen anyway."

"Good. I have in mind a rather long farewell."

"You could wake a dead man," Jack told her, as he gathered her in, war and Bogie and the past unimportant for the moment.

Chapter 5

An immense cavern. A world of mist and rain without, a clean rain, sprouts shooting upward at its touch, a pioneer world barely touched by civilization and unaware of the dangers of Thrakian sand. Yet, on the far side, a canker growing, an ever exacerbating sore, was the cause that drew this council in the cavern. A sleek, sable-coated humanoid paused before the cavern's maw, wiped his whiskered face neatly with supple hands and looked about. His only concession to clothing was a pair of slicker yellow shorts, bulging with various full pockets, and a tail slit for his sable appendage. He was one of the otter-folk, calling themselves Fishers, and this, their world, was meant to be one of mist and rain.

But it was the canker that drew them together. Skal was the last of the arrivees and, though he could hear the chatter of the bickering Elders within, he had little desire to join them. He looked out across the high plateau, across the mud flats and pastures blowing in the wind like seas of grass, and gave a sigh.

"Deep thoughts," said a husky Fisher voice at his back, and Skal swung about, his body a sinuous ribbon of movement, to face the female, her own sleek coat a rich and rare cream color, like the mystic fogs of their waterways.

"Yes, they are, Mist-off-the-waters," Skal answered. He patted her arm.

"They're waiting for you."

The younger, in his Fisher prime, gave a bob of his head. He knew well that he was the guest of honor. "Let's go in then. I'm as braced as I will ever be." He took a last deep breath of water-laced air, and headed into the cavern, his tail stiff and resolute behind him.

They did not chant or pass the pipe for him, and Skal was just as glad. He sat, nose down, unable to look in the eyes of his Elders, though every Fisher orb was luminescent as the moon, bright with anticipation. He gathered what it was he had to say, having come straight from the trading post with its subspace vid-screen, one of the planet's only links with civilizations far more advanced than theirs. He knew what it was the Elders were going to ask of him and, worse, he knew what answer it was he was going to make.

A one-armed Fisher, silver at his muzzle and ear tips the only blemish in his raven black pelt, broke off niceties with a grunt. "Let's quit farting around," he said in his deep-throated rasp. "We've a problem. Let's solve it."

Around the circle, russet, sable, and gray muzzles turned to him. Mist twitched a little and blinked, her blue-black eyes showing little white and a grave expression. "Trust One-arm to get to it quickly," she said, and gave a humorous Fisher shrug.

The youngest Fisher there, one who had earned the title Elder by virtue of her experience rather than her age, bore a remarkable scar. It was a laser burn, across her brow, pink tissue furrowing to ear tip, an alien scar from times they remembered but seldom spoke of. Her name was Little Fish and she gave a light, polite cough, before interrupting. "Someone had better speak," she said. "The wound at Three Falls widens daily. Men fester it like swamp bugs. Their poison grows to threaten us all. And, I'm told, twenty leagues south at Deep Hole, a cubling with two heads was born."

A hiss rumbled about the circle, tumbling the woodsmoke from the fire in its lazy curl to the ceiling.

"This cannot be true!"

"It is, I swear to you. I have seen it in the smoke myself. Poisons washed away from the wound fill the earth . . . soon the world."

"Off-worlder poison. . . ."

"Aiiii." One of the Elders rocked on her haunches, her arms over her head.

A black and russet muzzle hissed, "We must rid ourselves of them!"

One-arm growled. "I am right!"

Mist laughed softly, and the other Fishers turned to look at her in amazement, shock over the two-headed cub still in their eyes. She shook her head, curbing her feelings. "At last," she said. "We are all agreed on something!"

A thickly russet-coated male who had not spoken yet, leaned to his right, lifted a hind-leg and passed wind, before saying with a grunt, "Give Skal his assignment."

Mist nodded.

This was what Skal had feared, and he would not look up as the ivory female spoke to him.

"Bring back the Sun. Find the Warrior and bring him back to Mistwald. He showed us his might, and spared us from it. Now he must fight for us again."

The Fisher would not meet Mist's eyes as he said, "We cannot start a war with the off-worlders. We already know the price it would mean paying."

"Would you die from woundfester?"

Skal leaped to his feet. The pelt at the back of his neck bristled. That which had wounded him as though it were a hook or talon in his chest pricked at him now: the death of his once-foe, once-comrade. Hero to them, friend to him. He did not wish to speak of Storm's death, for it would crush the hopes of the Fisher-folk, but now he could not avoid it. "It cannot be done. He is dead! I myself saw the ceremonies across the stars when he was laid to rest."

Mist said softly, "Not so."

He met her gaze then, his own fierce brown eyes practically ablaze. "Ask any at the trading post. We watched it through the smoke screen from sub-space." He stammered to a halt then, his own emotions choking in his throat. "I brought him to you once, *but I cannot bring him to you again.*"

One-arm muttered, "We are lost. The poisons will spread. Can nothing be done?"

Mist got to her feet also, her tail lashing angrily from side to side instead of balancing her weight. She showed neat Fisher teeth as she barked out, "Will you give up, then? Never!"

Before the entire circle of Elders, she thrust her hand into the fire, deep into its red and orange flames, without a cry as the blaze angrily licked at her pelt.

When she drew her hand out, a small, carved knife lay in her palm, and she was untouched by the burning. "You gave the twin of this knife to Little Sun. If he were dead on Mistwald, what would happen to that knife?"

"It . . . would no longer exist."

"And this is the knife's soul. Does it exist?"

He stared at the object in her hand. "Yes, but—"

"Do not contradict me! You see the knife's soul!—it exists. Therefore, the knife exists, therefore Little Sun still lives! Find him, Skal."

A spear of hope lanced through him. "He's not on Mistwald."

Fat, burly Croaker laughed. "If he were, we would not have our deathwound opening up. You must go where the knife's soul takes you."

Skal looked about the cavern. Tallow candle stubs guttered low. Late afternoon had fled to deepest night outside, he could see the bowl of the sky, deepest velvet, star littered. "Even if it means off-world," he said, acquiescing to the council.

"Wherever it leads you," Mist answered, though he had not questioned. "Wherever."

Chapter 6

"No," Amber repeated softly. "I won't go with you." She tucked her chin in, and her hair fell about her face, shielding her expression. Silently, Colin watched both her and Jack, reserving his opinion for the moment.

"No? You're one of the main reasons I came back."

"Me ... and the Green Shirts. I'm not fool enough to think you can find them and protect me at the same time."

Jack stopped and rocked back on his boot heels, grinding down on the edge of the Walker reverend's priceless carpet. "You don't need protection."

"Damn right, but you'd try to give it to me anyway." The young woman added gently, "I would have given everything to go with you, but there's work to be done here. Duryea gave you a lead, one that you can't follow if you're going after the Green Shirts. If there is a countess, she won't be easy to tie in, and that means she won't be anywhere near where you're going to have to go."

"And where am I going?"

Amber looked from Jack to Colin and back

again. "Are you serious? You have to head for the Outward Bounds—the frontier is full of young rebels. One or two are bound to be the serious type."

Jack looked at Colin. "Did you tell her?"

The saint shrugged. "Did I have to? She just told you. The only thing she didn't tell you is that you're going to be using Bogie for the bait."

Amber shrank back in the chair, tucking her long legs under her. "Use Bogie? Oh, Jack."

"I haven't any choice. The wreckage at Gibbon's had been combed through—there's no sign of the two suits I had shipped there. Bogie's all I've got."

"What if they slit your throat and take him? He's just a baby."

"That baby is as bloodthirsty as most Thraks—and you know it." Jack scrubbed his hand through his sandy-colored hair. "I'll leave him half-powered and disconnect the deadman switch. That's about all I can do. And what about me, lying there with a slit throat?"

She wrinkled her nose. "I thought I taught you better. If not—" she broke off and gave an eloquent shrug.

"You can take the girl out of the street, but not the street out of the girl," Jack said to Colin.

The older man said nothing, but the fierce wrinkles at the corners of his mouth were testimony to the effort it took to restrain himself. Jack finished pacing, stopping at the far corner of the room.

"So once I'm at the Outward Bounds, where do I go?"

"The junkyard," Amber answered promptly. "The strip shops, the retreads. One flash of Bogie and you'll attract all the attention you want. From there . . ." She spread her hands.

"And as for you—"

"I'll keep an eye on her," Colin said abruptly.

She gave him a wise look. "You won't have to. Vandover will be watching out for me."

"Trouble?" Jack asked.

"Nothing I can't handle." She hid her fear with a toss of her head.

He knew better than to press her. If he had to leave her behind, he had to trust that both of them could handle it. He knew Colin well, and the older man would never knowingly let Amber come to harm. The Walker structure had a range almost as far-reaching as both the Dominion and Pepys' Triad Throne combined—and an admirable spy organization within it. If and when Vandover Baadluster came to conclusions about Amber, Colin would know about it almost as quickly as the Minister of War concluded it.

"How are you working your way toward the Outward?" Colin asked smoothly.

"The same way I got here. Odd jobs, hitchhiking. To do it any differently is asking for trouble once I've contacted the Shirts. They'll be able to monitor me since I 'died' on Colinada."

"Time's against you."

"I know. It might be quicker to go in as contract labor, but I'd have no control over where they'd send me and," here Jack smiled grimly, "I've an aversion to chilling down."

"Why not ship out on one of the Walker supply barges?"

That offer took Jack a moment to consider, then he shook his head. "Denaro's likely to have tapped into your freight lines—and since we're unsure at the moment where his loyalties lie, it wouldn't be safe for either of us."

"We haven't established that Denaro is working at cross-purposes."

"No," Jack said smoothly. "And I don't have time to wait while you do. It's not fair to him or your organization to start an inquiry now, anyway. You might create what you've been trying to avoid."

Quietly Amber said, "You could go freelance mercenary again."

Again, Jack shook his head. "Bogie's too conspicuous. If I go as a mechanic, he's just another trunk of tools. But I'd have to use him if I freelanced. Pepys would have me collared as soon as I applied for work. No. I think I know what I have to do."

Amber pushed herself out of the chair. The dark blue jumpsuit she wore tailored to her curves echoed the suppleness of her movement. "You know I don't like long good-byes, so I'll say them here and now." She looked intently at Jack. "You never promised me it would be easy, and I won't have you making stupid promises now. So I won't make you any either. Just do your best."

"You know I will—"

She turned away abruptly, bolting to the door. In the moment she waited for it to slide open, she blurted, "I know that. I also know it could get you killed one of these days," and the door let her out before he could answer.

Colin stood up and put his hand on Jack's arm, restraining him lightly. As Jack turned an accusing gaze on him, the man said gently, "Let her go. It's not safe for you beyond my apartment walls anyway."

They watched the door shut out the vision of Amber fleeing.

After a long moment of silence, Jack shrugged off his friend's hand. "That's not like her."

Colin turned away, gathering up his overrobe before seating himself once more. "Of course not," he said. "Jack, you're a straightforward man, and if you have any fault at all, it's that you deal with people on the same basis."

Jack sat opposite him. He leaned forward, tracing the redwood burl table with a blunt forefinger. "I'm riddled with faults," he said. "What's that got to do with it?"

"Amber was trained to be a child of subterfuge and you tend to forget that."

"Amber," Jack answered dryly, "was trained to be an assassin."

"Be that as it may, she bolted out of here so that you would not begin to question her about what her activities would be."

He stopped tracing the rings of life grown on a faraway planet and looked up, frowning. "What do you mean? She knows her way around under-Malthen. She knows how to access the information we need without causing trouble."

"Maybe. Maybe not."

"What do you mean?"

"The biggest source of information to tap here, or just about anywhere, is the emperor."

Colin had Jack's complete attention now. "Admittedly, Pepys has a web strung just about everywhere—for that matter, so do you."

"And he watches his enemies closely. Almost as closely as he watches his friends. She may inquire in under-Malthan, but I'm willing to wager she'll end up trying to tap Pepys' files."

Jack licked dry lips. "You'll be watching out for her?"

"Indeed, I will. And actively dissuading her from trying such a course. But I think it's important for you to know that you're not the only one at risk."

"I never thought I was."

There was a pause, then Colin nodded. "I should not have thought that of you, Jack." He rubbed one hand across the back of the other, soothingly. "I only pray that you all succeed." He stood up. "Before you leave, I'd like to show you something . . . something I didn't want Amber to view." He keyed on his large wall screen.

On edge, Jack sat back, wondering what the Walker was about to show him. The wall unit came on, and he recognized a recon satellite's view of a planet—a water planet, and he guessed he was watching one of the outer colonies.

"Thasia," Colin said. "Mainly inhabited by Walkers."

"Heard of it," Jack told him. "A dome world. Looks good, but the temperatures are a little extreme."

"That's it. It's far out. May never have been

suitable for massive colonization." Colin sighed as the recon focus brought the world in closer.

"Never have been . . ." Jack repeated.

"Watch," Colin told him.

And Jack did. Watched as the recon satellite, on the edges of its broadcast image, caught the fringe of an incoming fleet. A warship like nothing he'd ever seen before, and even as he said, "Who the hell's that?" to Colin, the view screen showed domes cracking like egg shells, the precious life they protected suddenly exposed to the hostile environment.

That attack was over in minutes.

Colin watched even after the screen darkened to black. "They never," he said, with great effort, "even got out an alarm. The satellite was destroyed on their way out."

If he expected a similar reaction from Jack, he didn't get it. Storm got to his feet and moved close to the wall unit. "Run that back again."

Colin, wide-eyed, opened his mouth as if to protest. Instead, he keyed out his request, and the video ran back. "Tell me when."

"All the way to the beginning." Jack watched intently as Thasia was destroyed. "Freeze it there."

Colin did so. Jack tapped the back of his hand on the screen. "No defense? Any word from Baadluster or Pepys?"

"No. But it's early yet. I should hear from Pepys tomorrow morning."

Jack looked back to the freeze-frame. "This was done by the Ash-farel."

"That was what we concluded."

"A Thrakian League wing was in that quadrant. They should have been in there, on defense."

Colin cleared his throat. "Unless the Ash-farel came through them first."

"Doubtful." Jack paced back and forth, his shadow momentarily interrupting the projection. He halted again. His forefinger stabbed the close-up of destruction. "I don't know who the hell they are, but we've been told a lot of lies about them."

"Lies? Lies?" Colin's voice went up a notch. "They've wiped out thousands of innocent people."

"And left the planet virtually untouched. They're fighting a 'Pure' war, Colin. That planet, in a year or three, will be perfectly habitable again. The Thraks have been lying to us about the kind of destruction and fighting the Ash-farel are doing."

"Lives, human lives—"

"Damnit, I know that! But we're not talking about total destruction. We're not talking about firestorming, like what happened to Claron. I'm a Knight, and we were trained to kill humans, flesh, war machines, whatever it took, like killing vermin—but always to leave the planet clean. Habitable."

Colin snapped the projection off, and the wall went dark. Jack stared at it for a moment longer, as if he could still see the image.

" 'Pure' war or not," his friend said, "they're killing us off. They can get through our defenses and the Thrakian defenses—and they won't be stopped."

Jack smiled then, a short, grim smile that made

Colin shiver. "But that's the key to them. They're not destroying the planets. They've a moral or ethical standard that we might even begin to understand, if we could contact them. And, whatever the Ash-farel are, the Thraks are afraid of them. Very, very afraid of them."

"And they fight a 'Pure' war."

"Exactly. It confirms my gut feelings—the reason I deserted my command. We may be allied with the Thraks in order to face the Ash-farel, but I think we're fighting the wrong enemy."

Colin's lips tightened. "That may be—but human lives, souls, are not vermin to be cleansed off a planet's surface."

"That all depends on your point of view," Jack answered.

Chapter 7

"Duryea's been reported dead, and his labs destroyed." Baadluster's tone of voice implied that he was not unhappy to be rid of the man.

Pepys did not stir in his communications web. He did roll an eye toward his somber Minister of War. "I know," he said shortly, as though part of him were listening to another voice—which it was.

"There was no record of the experiments he was conducting for you. You'll have to begin all over again."

"I know," the emperor repeated patiently. "What I don't know is who attacked him."

Baadluster gave a slight bow of acknowledgment, saying, "I've men working on it. If we can discover how the labs were blown—"

Pepys waved a negligent hand. "Forget it. Duryea destroyed them himself. I know his handiwork, seen it before. He doesn't like to leave evidence behind when he's forced to move. Particularly evidence that he might not get paid for."

"I see."

Pepys did stir then, rising from his chair and

removing his crown of probes. "As well you might." Released from its imprisonment, his red hair began to waver in the slight air currents caressing the room. "Tell me what you find out as soon as you can. The Green Shirts usually protect their own. This time they didn't. I want to know why."

Baadluster made a full bow this time, and turned to leave. His departure was interrupted by Pepys who made a loud noise, flung his arm out, and snapped his fingers for Vandover's attention. His cat-green eyes were fixed on the bank of monitors. He pointed a shaking finger at one.

"There! Just coming in, subspace relay. The Ash-farel are attacking." He pulled his crown of input leads and probes firmly onto his brow and, white-faced, sat down to watch. Vandover hovered at his side, knowing that he should be in the domain of his own board room to see this, but he stayed, also knowing his aides would be recording the broadcast.

Pepys sat transfixed for the brief duration of the action. Suddenly the satellite went out of commission, and the screen went to test pattern at the abrupt cessation of the signal. Pepys' hands whitened as he grasped the arms of his chair.

"What happened? Who's on the defense line there? Why were there no shields up?"

Vandover scanned the coord information on the bandline still riding the top of the monitor's screen. He said flatly, "That's a Walker colony, your highness. I would assume shielding was too expensive for such a modest population. The domes would have been enough—ordinarily."

"Damn." Skin over the whitened hands pulled taut until knuckles showed through, each an individual death's head. "How long can we keep this from Colin and his damned council?"

Vandover stretched his neck and scratched a tiny mole upon it reflectively. "In all likelihood, he already knows. His spies are at least as good as yours."

Pepys turned in his chair and eyed his minister with a baleful green stare. Vandover shrugged. He had told the truth. If the emperor started taking offense at the truth, there was little he could do. The emperor licked paper thin lips. "I want to know whose quadrant that was and how the Ash-farel got by—and if they survived, why."

"Your wish is my command," Vandover said ironically. He bowed deeply in his black robes, the better not to see Pepys' mouth flex bitterly at his words. He turned and was halfway out of the portal before he straightened, the better to hide his own elation.

Pepys slammed the portal shut fast, but Vandover had already eased through it. He caught not even a scrap of the man's elusive black robes.

The emperor sat back in his chair. The bank of screens before him showed a myriad of activity worlds over. Nothing interested him. None of them would show him what he really wanted to know. None of them could broadcast the future.

Chapter 8

Skal huddled against the counter as his prospective employer frowned and took the Traveler's disk Skal had paid much for—almost as much as if it had been a genuine passport instead of counterfeit. The human Skal faced dropped the disk into a reader and studied what his monitor displayed for him.

The pitted hull of an off-world ship in its cradle loomed behind them. All about them was the bustle of the port, barely dimmed by the wall of plastishield between it and them. The Fisher felt almost as though he was right in the midst of the cradles and ships, dodging hand trucks and cargo walks in order to be interviewed. But all that bustle was actually beyond the shield. In here, inside the monstrous domed hall, were cubicles of business. Skal's whiskers twitched. He could not have guessed at the liveliness of the trade here, inside a dome where Fishers were not allowed, even on this their own world.

A computer/printer rattled frantically to his right, on the other side of a wall which he could see over if he stepped up to it and pushed his muzzle atop. Although curiosity tickled his insides as though he'd swallowed a live fingerling, he dared not look. The cubicle next door housed a lawyer and his computer was researching/ creating a contract before the very eyes of his client. The machinery was similar but different from the computer at the trading post which not only sold goods but inventoried them. Still, Skal was pleased he had recognized the technology for what it was: he would hate to have sat waiting like a half-tailed cubling, muzzle twitching with never-to-be-sated inquisitiveness.

None of the cubicles had a ceiling; partial walls separated them but did not offer real privacy. Higher up the dome were the blister window office cubicles for true privacy. Up there was where Skal would rather be, but he would not spend all the funds he had for the price of his ticket at one time. He had no idea how far he might have to go to find Jack Storm. The yellow flake from his rivers was worth a certain amount. Just how much, he was not sure, but all metal, no matter how base, had a bargaining worth.

His prospective employer gargled in his throat. "According to this, I'm all but ordered to take you off-world, if you want to go. You've been appointed Ambassador-At-Large."

The very tip end of his proud tail moved slightly, but Skal did not worry that he had been unmasked as the deceiver he was. His brief association with humans had shown him that they were not adept at reading Fisher body language. Instead, he gave a half-bow. "True, but would you rather not get value for your passage? I'm prepared to work for the journey."

The human on the other side of the counter had a massively round face, like that of the full moon, and little hair to decorate it with except for bushy eyebrows that moved fluidly up and down as though they were hairy-bodied caterpillars. "You're in a hurry."

Skal smoothed down his whiskers with a right palm. "Of a certainty. I cannot wait for a liner. Besides, your vessel has an itinerary appealing to me."

The captain laughed. It was much the same as his gargle, but louder. "I run a garbage scow!"

"You, sir, haul a scrap barge. You go where technology lives off its own carrion. You may not have noticed, but—" and here Skal leaned forward confidentially, "Mistwald is a low-technology world." A shiver of apprehension ran its way through his deep sable coat, mottled with amber dapples. If he was not taken on now, he would have to wait until after the barge cleared port before he dared show his disk around again. It would be a terrible delay if that came to pass.

An eyebrow arched, fatly and proudly. "I thought you Fishers liked it that way."

"I might remind you that the Dominion rejected us, not vice versa."

Captain Obe sat back in his chair. He had been leaning on his plump elbows on the counter. He smiled. "Now I understand. You not only want a trip, you want an education. Well. Scrap boy doesn't pay much—"

Skal shrugged, an eloquent Fisher shrug which rippled his supple body all the way to the tip of his foot claws. "I don't ask much," he said, and opened his muzzle in a wide grin.

Rain left under-Malthen stinking instead of cleansed, damp and mildewed. Piles of garbage that occasionally mummified and disintegrated into dust to blow away were now rotten and putrefied. Welcome, Amber thought, to the rainy season. Jack's funeral and brief visit seemed a lifetime ago, in the few days of storm that preceded the actual rain by several weeks. She slogged through the gutter, clutching a light plastic wrap about her body, her hair tucked in under its hood. Without seeming to, her body wove a pattern along the sidewalk, eluding most of the views of the security cameras. Old habits died hard.

A light hand skittered over her buttock. Amber whirled, spotted the wide-eyed child, and snarled, "Beat it, Skag!" and pivoted again so quickly that she caught the real perp by his wrist, trying to pick her waist belt. The boy's lip curled in a grimace.

"Amateur night," Amber told him, and thrust his arm away from her, freeing him. "Wait for the streets to fill up."

The teen spat out, "Nobody's out today."

"They'll be out. You've just got to know when the traffic flows. Learn what you're doing." Amber moved swiftly again and caught the first child, a girl, probably, his sister, in the midst of trying to pick her boot shank. "You two just don't give up, do you?" she asked, her fingers entwined in the child's greasy hair.

The girl gave a yelp, but her partner merely shrugged. "Times is rough," he said.

Amber nodded. "Times *are* rough." She dropped a five credit bit in his hand. "Get some hot food."

They bolted so fast that the girl left hair wrapped in Amber's fingers. She stood pensively on the sidewalk, in the darkening light, and shook the strands free on the wind. Times were rough. She'd made Jack promise her years ago that he'd never bring her back to under-Malthen, but here she was, of her own volition, living in hell.

With a shudder, she began to walk again, seeking the neighborhood of her old apartment. Better here than in the barracks, where Vandover Baadluster made no apology for the shameless recording of everything she did and everything she said. And there was a bank of charlatan psychics working in the palace for Pepys who would have liked to have reported on everything she thought as well. When she'd lived with Jack, she'd gotten away with jamming the cameras and mikes, but now she knew she walked a thin line between what Pepys would allow and what he wouldn't.

As for the psychics, so few had any real talent at all that she'd never had to shield her powers. As for now ... with the power burned out of her, she no longer had to worry. Not that Baadluster had given up hunting her. No, even though the war effort diverted his attention, he would be locating her soon enough. Amber made a mental note to move again this weekend. She'd keep Baadluster guessing as long as she could. That was not psychic intuition—it was common sense.

Her wrap tangled about her knees as she turned the corner to catch the back lift to her rooms. She stumbled and caught herself against the rough siding of the building. Her breath stuttered in her chest. She pulled back into the shadows, lower lip caught in her teeth as she stifled her surprise.

Like a bitter wind piercing her, she had caught a flicker of presence in her rooms. A rank, low, and muttering presence. Baadluster.

He had already caught up with her.

Amber hugged herself as she went cold in that bitter wind. He would be at the window, watching for her. It had been pure luck that she'd caught scent of him first. No, not luck ... the last, burning flicker of her psychic abilities. She eased past the edge of the building and looked up. A shadow briefly interrupted the golden glow of the interior lights. She'd left them on, knowing it would be dark when she returned. Left them on as proof against just such an intrusion as she now faced. The shadow moved. Vandover, pacing in his impatience. One of the few traits he shared with Jack.

She hesitated only a second longer, as she decided where she would go now. Yes—the labor district, on the edge of the border between Malthen proper and its shadier environs. A favorite housing for the high-priced technicians, particularly hospital techs, who could not quite afford the best. Pepys would not look for her to move closer. Besides, she had exhausted her connections in this part of the city. It might be more convenient to be closer. She might find herself with her own hands in the emperor's pockets, so to speak.

The sky grew completely dark, and a shower began pelting out of the oppressive cloud cover. She left in its protection.

Chapter 9

Jack woke for a second time that night, the stale taste of failed *mordil* rank in his mouth. He reached out instinctively, but the anti-grav hammock had him securely and he wasn't going anywhere accidentally. Someone made a noise in his sleep, and Jack stilled, aware that they were packed in close quarters and his restlessness would easily be transmitted.

He laid his head back, pillowed it on his left hand. The small vial of *mordil* could be felt in one of his left leg pockets, like a thorn pressing in. He wouldn't take any more tonight. Sleep would come or it wouldn't. Either way, he was accustomed to it now. After seventeen years of involuntary cold sleep, his body refused to let normal sleep come quietly. He was used to the phenomenon by now and getting addicted to *mordil* wasn't any more attractive than being awake.

He'd been dreaming of Claron—wild and unsettled, new frontier, as he'd enjoyed it before the firestorming. He'd dreamed of the damned rascally boomrats and their persistent raids on the brewery malt fields. Somewhere in his gear lay a shiny green stone, a pebble really, left in barter by one of the wily boomrat gang leaders. Had any of the creatures managed to survive the firestorming? By any stretch of the imagination, could he picture their warrens deep enough underground to resist the heat and flame? That they would have been the type of animal to lay aside stores of grain and nuts against future shortages of food? Could there be life stealing back into Claron even though he had failed to persuade Pepys to terraform what was left? If so, it would mitigate a few of his nightmares.

Lying there, he became aware of the stench of the barracks—of rancid sweat and unwashed bodies. He caught a whiff of *ratt*. Now there was a drug he stayed as far away from as he could. So did anyone with half a brain. He thought he could pinpoint who was using it and made a note to stay away from the man on work details. He would be violent and paranoid and erratic—any one of which could get a man killed on a staggering old vessel like the one they rode.

The *New Virginia* had, at one time, been a proud warship, but now was a gutted hull outfitted to run the most cargo—be it agra, flesh, or scrap—it could hold. Amenities were a luxury on any warship, and light-years away from this one. She creaked when she made FTL, shuddered when she turned the corner coming out of FTL. Pipes throbbed whenever anyone turned on the water and the heads damn near flushed directly into deep space. Her pitted outer skin shed heat tiles like dandruff every time they spun into a landing orbit. And Jack wouldn't have been on her if he'd had any place better to go.

The *New Virginia* was only slightly better than shipping out chilled down as contract labor. Besides his aversion to cold sleep and cold sleep fever, there was the added disadvantage of being unable to control his downtime. He might be shipped out and awakened in three months—or three years. Assuming, of course, the Thraks and Ash-farel had left anything behind of the human-held worlds in three years.

A spindly hand grabbed through the hammock netting and caught his ankle. It jolted him out of his thoughts. "Asleep, m'boy?"

Jack fought the recoil reflex. "No," he said softly.

"Didn't think so. Out of there, m'boy, and come sit my hand for me." The viselike grip loosened and Jack peeled out of his hammock netting to swing down to the deck.

He landed cat-light, leaving other sleepers in their dreams as he joined Heck by the bulkhead. In the twilight illumination of the corridor beyond, the elder man looked more skeletal than ever. His twisted height barely reached that of Jack's shoulder yet the impact of his personality was such that few disobeyed Heck's oblique requests. Storm was used to commanding presences from his time in the military. He obeyed Heck when he felt like it. Tonight was such a night. A game of cards would be a pleasant diversion when stacked against nightmares.

Heck peered up at him, dim light reflecting in the yellow-white of his eyes.

"Good game?" Jack asked, stepping past him into the corridor.

"Fair enough," Heck answered. He scratched a rooster-comb thatch of gray hair. "Bet what you like—but if you've made a dent of more than fifty credits in my winnin's, I want it repaid."

Jack nodded his understanding as Heck led him along the cluttered walkway to the galley, the only place with enough room for recreation. Heck was Stop boss. He still wore his greasy coveralls from the day shift and the suit hung from his bone-thin frame.

"Taking a break?"

Heck nodded as they approached the galley. "Stamina ain't what it used to be, but I won't let *them* know it"

Jack felt a grin tug at the corner of his mouth. Heck must be playing with the flight officers again, hence the automatic siding of "us against them." As one of the mechanic crew members, Jack found himself in a decidedly under strata layer of respect on the *New Virginia*. It was about the only circumstance that could make allies of Jack and Heck.

Heck threw back scrawny shoulders and sauntered into the galley, calling out, "This here's Jack. He'll be sittin' in for me while I make my constitutional."

MacGrew, Jack recognized him as one of the navigating staff, threw back his head and snorted a laugh. "Constitutional, hell. Old man, you're going to take a nap"

"Maybe I am and maybe I'm not." Heck pulled

out a rickety chair for Jack to sit in. "But this boy's going to hold my place. Any objections?"

MacGrew pointed a blunt finger saying, "You just heard one—" but his voice was overrun by the other three at the table muttering their approval. MacGrew sat back, his heavy face flushing. Jack straddled the chair and their eyes met, and then MacGrew grinned.

He shrugged as if in apology for his temperament. As the deal went round, Jack caught up a handful of cards, their plastic edges frayed and brittle. Heck stayed a moment, pacing back and forth behind him.

MacGrew looked up, but it was the young, pale-haired, dark-eyed officer next to him who said, "Go ahead, Heck, beat it. And get something to eat while you're at it. I can't stand looking at those bones of yours."

Heck cackled obscenely, then added, "Fun me all you want, boys—but when the Thraks come get us, they won't be eatin' *me!*" He left to further hoots of derision, knobby back stiff.

Only Jack was silent, staring after him. Only Jack and the men who'd been with him on a disastrous run at a Thrakian sand crèche knew that the Legion kept humans as fodder for their larvae. Where in the hell had Heck been, and how much did he know?

The pale-headed officer tapped his shoulder. "Let's go, Jack. I haven't got all night to get my money back. Ante up."

With difficulty, he wrenched his thoughts back to the cards.

*   *   *

Even with FTL, it would be a few weeks before they landed dirtside at the most likely of the Outward Bounds' retread shops. Jack knew he would have to take his time and stalk Heck patiently, or the canny old man would avoid him entirely, Shop boss or not. His suspicions were validated the next shift when he found his stint traded arbitrarily for another shift. Staring a game wouldn't get him closer to Heck, so Jack spent most of his work period shifting through ideas on how to isolate him effectively without scaring him off.

A tone sounded and the lights flashed. Jack looked up, then massaged the back of his neck. He was on free time now. He cleaned up his workbench, keyed in the equipment he'd left soaking in a mild acid bath for the next shift, and looked around to find himself alone. The swing shift was a fairly solitary work period. Squaring his shoulders, Jack slapped his palm against the portal lockplate and waited to be let out as the lights dimmed down.

A jackhammer slammed against his collarbone, and he was lifted off his feet, then dragged sideways. Jack went limp as the fabric about his neck drew taut. He recognized the half-wheeze of the man who had him even as he coiled for a strike. Surprise kept him still as the old man dragged him into a side bulkhead with amazing strength.

As the fabric went slack and the grip loosened, Jack pulled himself to his feet. He towered over Heck, who seemed suddenly reduced.

Heck stuffed a handful of credit disks into Jack's hand. "You're share of th' winnings, m'boy."

He wheezed three quick breaths, then gulped hard, as if trying to steady his breathing. He looked up, and there was a feral glint in his yellowing eyes. "They all laugh at me, allus have. But you didn't. You hide it real well, boy, but I *saw*. It was in your eyes. You knew what I meant, didn't you? Who the hell are you?"

Jack looked down at the old man. Probable answers ran through his mind, and he discarded most of them. He said, "What does it matter who I am?"

Heck fairly shook with agitation. "They laugh at me. They know nothin' about the Thraks. You do. How? Have you seen what I've seen?" He pointed at his bleary eyes, hand cocked as if he held a palm laser.

"Let them laugh," Jack told him. "They don't know."

"But you do."

Jack looked down at the bony man. Just how old was he, under that skin like leather? "Maybe."

"Don't jack me around, boy!" Heck seemed to shoot upward in height, as he straightened and threw his jaw forward. "You might be found floatin' in one of them acid baths come morning shift."

Jack stepped out of the bulkhead frame. He drew himself up, taking the same stance he would if he were wearing armor, a presence he had not allowed himself to exhibit for weeks. Fear was suddenly mirrored on Heck's face. He stepped back involuntarily as Jack said softly, "Is that a threat?"

"Now, now. Don't be hasty. We're all of us

salvage on this heap o' scrap. No last names, no questions. There's metal in you I didn't see before, that's for sure. I spoke out of turn."

"Now that you see it, listen. I've fought Thraks. When and where is unimportant. What's important is that we both know part of the secret lying behind those beetle-masks. I intend to find out the rest—you can tell me, or not. I'll find out one way or another."

The will that puffed Heck up evaporated. The old man sank into himself, seeming even smaller than usual. He sagged against the bulkhead for support, hooking an elbow over a massive bolt to keep himself upright. "It's a long story," the Shop boss capitulated.

"I don't sleep much on my rest shift anyway."

"And it's not a pretty story," Heck continued as though not hearing Jack. "M'boys—if they'd lived, would be about forty now. We were Treaty breakers, an' with the Alliance now, what's left of my life is forfeit if anyone ever finds out."

The corridor lights dimmed and stayed low as Heck told his story. He and his three sons were scavengers ... salvagers with little sense of duty or obligation. They made their living taking the pickings from the planets the Thraks had conquered ... combing the sands to salvage the installations left behind by the original colonies and the military. They had outfitted a light corsair to stay one step ahead of the Thraks, and under cover of the newly negotiated treaty between the Thrakian League and the Dominion and the Triad Throne, which once again gave the Thraks access to the major trade lanes, the sand planets were not closely monitored. Humans shunned them. They were wide open for the kind of hit and run salvage techniques Heck and his three sons practiced.

Jack felt the hair crawl on the back of his neck as the Shop boss described their various deeds. A planet conquered and disintegrating into Thrakian sand was not a pretty sight—but he'd had no idea of the parasites like Heck who crawled over it, picking and plucking at the carcass with its precious bits of life left. He felt no sympathy for the man who now described the growing and inevitable Thrakian awareness of what they were doing.

It was greed that led to their downfall. Stupidity, too, Jack told himself and tried not to reflect that in his expression. But Heck wouldn't haven't noticed. He was too wrapped up in his tale of woe, and in the loss of three proud sons.

Though they hadn't been proud when they were captured by the Thraks. No. They had offered the worth of their cargo and corsair for their freedom. But since the Thraks had already taken that, they had nothing with which to bargain. The Thraks were interested in something else.

Heck sighed. "That something we didn't know until we were taken to th' larder camp, near the Windshears."

The sentence lanced through Jack, as though he'd been half asleep and was now chillingly awake. "Where?"

Heck smirked. "You wouldn't a-heard of it, m'boy. It's on Milos, and nary a man's come back alive since we lost it to the Thraks."

"What is it? An installation?"

"Naw. A mountain range, so sharp-edged to a hellacious wind that it damn near slices it—and aircraft comin' in there—in half." Heck rubbed his eyes wearily as if the talk was slowly draining him of what life he had left.

Jack hoped the movement would hide the tumble of emotions racing through him. He and K'rok had survived Milos ... separately, although the Milots had called in the Dominion Knights to ally with them in the ground war. Jack was one of the few who had made it to transport. The ground sweep had been a rout. He was not sure if he wanted to hear the fate of even a few of the forces stranded by orders given by a young Pepys, even then in search of emperorhood.

"Not that that bothered the Thraks. They snugged right up against th' foot of the Windshears and started making sand. M'boys and I were marched in to join the rest of the food supplies. We had hopes of getting out, though. Thraks like their meat as fresh as they can get it. My sons were all big, brawny bucks, but the Thraks thought they could fatten up my bones a little, too. There was two cold sleep transports just outside th' base, buried up to their launch cradles in sand, but we thought—we planned—to get inside and see if we could take them up."

"Transports?"

"That's what I said. Grounded as plain as anything, for all the sand drifted over their hulls."

The implications of what the old man told him washed over Jack. Cold ship transports had been grounded instead of lifting troops off Milos— leaving thousands of men and hundreds of Knights to the enemy. Grounded at Pepys' command, given through the now-dead officer Winton. But any ship kept an automatic computer log, a bank, of its instructions, the infamous black box, the origins of which were now lost in legend. If Jack could get to such a ship, and if it had not been stripped by the Thraks, he would have in his hands proof of the betrayal perpetrated by Winton and Pepys in order to gain an emperor's throne. It would mean going back to Milos—back to where his nightmares had begun. "But you didn't make it," he said, and got a grip on his thoughts.

"No. They picked us off one by one. I got out because I was the only one left—I was always the wiry sort. I stole a hover and got picked up by another scrapper. Had to leave my last boy behind, meat for the grubs like the rest."

Heck took a wavery breath. "What's the matter, boy? You look a little peaked. Did you think that Milos would die a cleaner death than th' rest?" Heck gave a harsh bark of a laugh. "Nothin' those bugs do is clean. No. We found our boys hanging from meathooks in ice caves underground, just waiting for the nest to warm up enough for—"

"I know," Jack said flatly, cutting him off. The tone of his voice made Heck pause and clear his throat as though thinking whether to venture further and not.

Finally, with an unsteady hand completely

leeched of the strength it had earlier, Heck touched his arm. "You've seen it, too."

"I have." Jack took a cleansing breath, then added, "You'd be wise to forget it."

"How can I?" Heck asked in a piercing whisper. "*How can I*? There's no one about with the balls to tell the truth anymore. Pepys all but sleeps with the Thraks, and the Dominion trots behind on his leash. Even th' Green Shirts lay down and died, ever since the Liberator disappeared . . . now all they do is take piss-ant bites out of Pepys whenever they can."

"Liberator?" repeated Jack.

"Oh, don't raise your eyebrows at me, pup. There was a day, about th' time you were born, when the Green Shirts were a glorious group. I hung on their jet stream for a while, but I wasn't good enough for them. I don't know who the man was who headed them, but his tag was Liberator, and he had balls enough for the whole lot of 'em. He's been gone twenty years or so now . . . and so has the heart of the movement. There was a day, boy, when scum like me wasn't good enough for them, and that's the way it shoulda stayed." Heck turned and began to shuffle away. "That should give you something to think about."

Jack watched him leave, fading into the grayed shadows of the old ship. Something to think about. Indeed. None of it pleasant.

Chapter 10

Vermin was too good a word to describe the inhabitants of Victor Three. They lived off a boiled scab of a world that even the shipbound crew didn't care to visit. Heck was the only one who cared enough to walk Jack off the *New Virginia*. They both took a look around the port— it had the look of having been strafed or firebombed and Jack wondered if they'd had a berthing accident or crash. Haphazard reconstruction was going on, while the existing concrete walls were black shadowed from the heat that had seared them.

Heck stopped, sucking at a tooth. "Strafed," he said, as if that explained it all.

"Who by?"

"Pepys, probably. No reason not to. Victor's a freebooters' planet. Doesn't hurt to remind 'em now and then who's the real boss." The Shop boss seemed even more shriveled than usual, as if his talk with Jack had bled him of whatever will to live he possessed, and he wheezed with every breath. At the berth's edge, he paused while Jack fetched a hand truck and loaded Bogie's trunk onto it.

He eyed the container. "Must be quite a collection of tools."

"It is." Jack dropped the trunk on the platform as gently as he could and programmed it to follow him at random.

"Must be a sight to see. Never seen a lock like that for tools."

"Probably not." Jack squinted, looking the port over. It was sloppy—vessels slipping in their berths, repair crews leaving equipment in aisles that ought to be kept clear, thrust pads dirty.

Heck scrubbed a callused hand over the front of his overalls. "What are you lookin' for here?"

Jack turned back to him. He let a faint smile come out. "Whatever I can find."

The old man spat to one side. It pooled in a puddle of grease. "You're no mechanic, m'boy. You're good—too good. You work on equipment as if your life depended on it, not your job."

He looked down, meeting the rheumy gaze. "You never complained before."

"It's a closed ship on board. What comes in, eventually goes out. I covered for you—but you'll never make it here. Too slow, too thorough. They'll cut you down to scrap."

"Who says I plan to stay?"

Heck hunched up a shoulder. "Well, that's it, ain't it," he responded. "You're too good for hereabouts, and they've got you spotted. Already, I'd say."

Jack watched the slidewalks as the crew pulled the joining ramps into place for loading and unloading. He felt an itch between his shoulder blades, a familiar feeling, as though the enemy already had him in their grid. He wished he was wearing his armor instead of trucking it. He looked back at Heck, who was scuffling his boots on the pad. "If I asked you for advice, would you give it?"

The old man looked up greedily. "Been a lot of years since a boy asked my advice." His faded eyes brimmed. "It depends on what you're looking for."

Jack decided to go for broke. "The Green Shirts."

Heck recoiled a step. Then a crafty expression passed over his seamed face. "Show me what you've got stowed in there, and I just might be able to point you in the right direction."

Jack let himself hesitate a fraction of a second, then he went down on one knee beside the massive trunk. Heck crowded against his shoulder. Jack shielded the trunk's combination, a triple keying sequence, and opened the lid very slightly.

Bogie lay quietly in the compartment, Flexalinks glimmering in the dim light of the port. The battle armor was on its back, legs bent and knees drawn up to fit in the trunk, helmet resting on the stomach of the equipment. Jack snapped the lid shut as Heck sucked in a wavery breath.

The old man narrowed his eyes. "That's armor!" he spat out, his voice barely above a whisper.

Jack made no motion other than to straighten up. "I'm waiting," he said calmly.

Heck made a physical effort to restrain himself. Finally, in a choked voice, he said, "Skagboots'. It's the only shop I know of where you can find what you want. Not that it's the only place, mind you—but the only one I know of for sure. Mind your step, m'boy. They'll slit your throat for that." He gave a jerky nod toward the trunk.

"I know." Jack held his hand out in farewell. The Shop boss stared at it a moment, uncomprehending, then reached out and took it.

The old man's clasp was deathly cold.

The city outside the port was gray as slate, dirty and unwashed, littered with garbage too precious to recycle and too worthless to repair. Jack skirted his way through the prefab sheds, some for storage and some blinking with the strobelike flare of welding lasers, shops too small to stand up straight in. Trash ought to be as colorful as the people who discarded it, he thought, but the scrap here on Victor Three was drab and pitted. Warehouses leaned against one another, with no thought of fire walls and noise ordinances. Their ribbed bulk all but hid a light blue sky, striped with the charcoal exhaust of smokestacks.

The hand truck rattled behind him, staying where it was programmed to, in spite of all the obstacles to foot traffic. Jack tried to walk through as though he did not know he was being observed, palm resting on the butt of the handlaser he had holstered at his right hip. The flickering weld-lights would pause a moment as his shadow darkened doorways, and then begin again.

He did not begin his search until he was through the fringe areas of the retread shops—he was not looking for penny-ante operations. When the industrial buildings grew big enough to blot out the sky, he became interested.

A live sentry leaned indolently in the frameway of the first shop he approached. It was automatic that here, among the scrapyards, human labor would be cheaper than robotic. Robotics were a byproduct of their labor—humans arrived here daily like so much flotsam from the rest of the Outward Bounds. The man looked as if he had never seen a comb, and his application of second-rate depilatory left a permanent day-old scrub of beard that looked tough enough to use for filings. He looked up diffidently as Jack approached, but the man missed nothing, not even the complaining hovers of the hand truck as it endeavored to keep its cargo afloat. Greed surfaced in the sentry's hazel eyes.

"What can I do for you, boss?"

The hand truck stopped at Jack's heels, literally nudging the backs of his calves. "Looking for work," Storm answered.

The sentry's gaze brushed over the trunk. "Delivering or employment?"

"Employment."

Interest died down a bit. The sentry rasped a thumbnail along the underside of his jaw. "Nothing here, boss. Labor's cheap."

"I have my own tools."

The sentry raised an upper lip, showing teeth in what might have been a smile. "There won't be any work here—probably not in all of Victor Three. You're too clean—which means you're trouble. You're here because you have to be. Want some advice?"

Jack's eyebrow went up, but he stayed silent, giving assent.

"Sell your tools and catch the first shuttle out. You're going to lose 'em anyway, might as well get some money for them."

"Lose them?"

The sentry leaned back against the framework of the factory doorway. "Lose 'em—or have 'em taken from you. It's all the same."

"Not to me. I'd have to be dead first."

"Wouldn't be the first time," the sentry returned. He shrugged. "Talk is cheap."

Jack palmed a credit disk and showed it. The afternoon sun, from somewhere behind towering buildings and smokestack exhausts, struck a glint in it. "Maybe not."

They clenched hands over the disk. Jack let the other pry it from his fingers.

The sentry tucked it in a secure pocket. "Well," he said. "I like a man who knows what a finder fee is. What are you looking for?"

"Skagboots'."

Fear abruptly washed the greed out of the other's eyes. "A couple of clics east. You can't miss it. Look for the mural on the side, called 'A Thraks Crucifixion.' "

The other's discomfort brought a tight smile to Jack's face as he said, "Sounds distinctive."

"It is." The sentry stuck a thumb in the portal lock, keying it. It slid open just wide enough to admit him, and he disappeared from Jack's sight.

As Jack turned about to sight his direction, he noticed that the sun was beginning to drop to the horizon, and that purple shadows were lengthening rapidly. He snapped his fingers to bring the hand truck about, and began walking east.

The scrap shops gave way to a junkyard, heavily fenced with sonic posts as well as wire. The yard seemed to be one continuous unit, hinting at a scrap operation far bigger than any he'd seen yet. There was heavy equipment here, tractor tows and berthing cradles, even a corsair, laser scarred and deepspace pitted, at rest among the mundane scrap of businesses and households. The size of the junkyard forced him to skirt it, unable to approach Skagboots' directly—unless this was part of Skagboots'. The thought instilled a certain amount of healthy respect in Jack.

A ragged purple shadow nearly hidden among the other shadows kept pace, and Jack finally separated the creature from its cover—a lumbering, man-sized lizard, with four hind legs to walk on and rather fearsomely clawed front legs at the ready at its chest. It raised its shovel head from time to time to look at him, and Jack knew he was looking at the equivalent of a junkyard dog. He wondered if the beast was a denizen of Victor Three or imported.

He also decided he wasn't going to get close enough to find out. The fencing and sonics were discouragement enough for him.

His stomach was grumbling by the time he reached the corner of the fencing and could see workers in the yard, scratching among the junk, selecting a bit here and there and tossing it onto slidewalks that led into a maw in the building's flank. Jack watched for a moment, thinking that he was hungry and thirsty, even as he tried to determine what motivated the selection of junk. There were no criteria that he could see. Beyond, bottom framed and fringed by towers of scrap, he could see the mural the sentry had told him of. It was not a pretty picture.

His stomach clenched fitfully. It had been a long time since he'd had a decent meal, and the *New Virginia* had not held a mess for departing employees.

The hand truck nudged at his calves again, faithful mechanical dogs, and whined under protest at the trunk's weight. Jack strode toward the front gates. They were open, the gateposts installed with monitors showing various videos about buying and selling scrap, or having repair work done, on a front monitor. Uninterested, he brushed past.

"Hey!" The Sentry camera lens snaked out, eyed him closely, and recoiled back into its station. "What are you doing?"

"I'm looking for Skagboots'."

"No Unauthorized Personnel."

Jack gave his tight smile, said, "Tell him Pepys sent me," and kept on walking.

That should bring some action at the front door.

He signaled the hand truck to flank him and keyed open Bogie's lock as he walked up the slight incline to the front shop doors. Underfoot, old plastic, brittle and broken, crunched beneath his boots. He could smell lubricant and cleansers, pungent on the air. He saw the remains of several hand trucks littering the path, and the machine flanking him made a chuffing sound as if headed toward the same fate, or in recognition of cold workmates. He stopped at the doors and saw himself reflected in the skin. Gone was the workman's demeanor adopted over the last several months, ever since he and Colin had fabricated his death. He stood tall and aggressive in front of Skagboots' monitor and dared them to come get him.

There was a flurry of sound on the other side, and when the door slid open, he looked into the muzzle of a good-sized rifle. The owner snarled, "What do you mean Pepys sent you?"

"This," and Jack kicked open the lid of his trunk.

The late afternoon sun caught the dazzle off the Flexalinks. It shone in the trunk as though made of white-fire, and the rifle holder flinched back a step, to shade his eyes. "Where in the hell did you get that?" issued from deep in the burly man's chest.

"Now that would be telling if I told you, and then we'd both know, and then you wouldn't have to talk to me to find out."

The man spat out an invective, then half-turned in the doorway. "Boots! Bootsie, c'mere!"

Bootsie was a robust woman, her chalk-fire hair pulled back in a tail, her lean hips and oversized bust filling a jumpsuit the way a sausage filled its casing—tight and appetizing. She stopped behind her guardsman, put her hands on her hips and eyed him with appraisal, aqua eyes outlined with kohl and sapphire powder. She paused when she looked into the trunk, then said, "Call in the crew and close the gates down."

"It's not dark yet."

"Do as I said." Bootsie gave Jack a dazzling smile. "I'd invite you in, honey, but we're not secure yet."

"I'll wait," he answered. She had a perfume that he could not identify. It was not overpowering, but definitely unique, underscented with pheromones because her presence was stirring his senses in a way that only Amber could. But Bootsie cheated.

Jack held onto his small smile and waited.

Chapter 11

He could not see all of the crew that gathered, but his neck hairs let him know he was being targeted from all directions, despite the stacks and vats and shelving that filled the warehouse vastness beyond Bootsie. Barrels of wire and tubing overflowed onto the ground as though the building were some great, disemboweled animal. Jack could hear Bogie's deep tones rumbling through his mind.

Boss, you in trouble?

"Not yet," Jack answered back, and sized up the forces, seen and unseen, answering Bootsie's summonings.

From above, high in the cubicles hung down from the rafters, a tinny voice called, "What's up, Boots?"

"Secure for strafing," she yelled back, without taking her large, emphasized eyes from Jack.

The air filled with the rumble of fire doors being closed—all but the doorway Jack stood in. He had no doubt that the gates down the lane were now shut and locked. A small wave of panic washed through him, that he had gone too far, naked as he was without his armor, but he ignored the fear as soon as he recognized it.

Yet he could not silence the echo in his mind: *Shit. We're in trouble now.*

Besides the rifleman, four sweat-streaked workers moved up to flank Bootsie. Any one of them looked pumped up enough to attempt lifting the equipment trunk and heaving it across the warehouse. They eyed him, various weaponry trained in his direction. Jack half-raised an open palm but refused to give way.

Bootsie cocked a coal-black eyebrow. "Well, you've got a foot in the door, as they say."

Her rifleman grunted, "They also say, move it or lose it."

Jack shook his head. "I'm here to do business, but if the deal falls through, I want to know you have an open door policy. This way I'm ensuring it."

Noises of equipment moving in the rafters drew a flicker of his attention. He could see movable cranes in motion along their tracks. One of the hooks came to a stop overhead.

Bootsie smiled. "Now we're secure, honey. Let's talk."

Jack shrugged. "I'm not much for talking. You've seen what I've got. Either you're interested or not."

She stretched, a languid movement that rippled muscles Jack didn't know women had. She looked overhead at the massive hook and then back. "I don't know what you've got until I see it. You could have it gutted and nothing but the shell there. Let's bring the cherry picker down and hoist it for a look-see."

Jack kicked the lid down, saying, "Let's not." Mentally, he told Bogie to be prepared to be up and running if anything happened to him.

The rifleman gave a snorting laugh and added, "This guy a virgin or something?"

The shop echoed with crude humor. Jack rode it out, his gaze staying level with Bootsie's. She did not smile until the noise died down. When she did smile, it was a cold stretching of wide, sensuous lips, an expression that did not warm her eyes.

"All right," she said. "All right, what do you want?"

"I'm looking for the Shirts."

The warehouse grew cavernously quiet. Jack thought he heard the woman's heart skip a beat, then quicken.

"And the suit is just a tease. Bait." Bootsie turned on one well-heeled boot, her hip jutting out at him.

"No tease," he said to her before she walked away from him. "I intend to wear it for the Shirts."

She gave him a look over her shoulder. "And you think we know where to find them?"

"Now who's being coy?"

The woman stopped in her tracks again, and swiveled about. Her gaze fixed greedily on the hand trunk and its cargo. "Suppose we do know how to find the parties you're looking for. What's in it for us?"

He shrugged. "I'll leave the building standing."

There was a sharp hoot from the rear. Bootsie put up a finger, and the laughter quieted. She paced slowly about Jack and the trunk, eyeing both very carefully. He had no doubt that she was memorizing every detail she saw. She halted when she was back in front of him.

"All right," she said. "I can find the Shirts for you."

He shook his head. "Not good enough."

Her face paled almost enough to match her platinum hair. "What do you mean, not good enough?"

"Let's drop the pretenses. My contact was taken out before I could find out where to go and who to see—but I got your name instead. I'm here with a suit, a suit that can be duplicated, in time, to meet Pepys on his own ground. Or do you prefer taking daily target practice from him? Last I saw, the port had been hit and it's only four clics from here. That doesn't exactly put you out of ground zero range if Pepys decides to stop toying with you. He'll stop discouragement and go right to annihilation once he finds out Skagboots' is the place he's been looking for."

The rifleman put him in his sights. His lip lifted as he said, "You ain't gonna tell him."

"Stop it," Boots said. She looked down, staring at the ground, as though she could read an oracle scratched in the dust. Then, with a sigh, she beckoned Jack out of the doorway. "Come on in. I personally guarantee safe passage out of here. But we can't talk until the door's closed down. It's too risky."

Jack eyed her. "Suit, too."

"Suit, too. Now come on in, mister, and don't be shy. Word is, there's going to be another run late today, and we don't want our asses hanging out in the breeze, do we, honey?"

The rifleman introduced himself as Gus. As the rest of the crew faded back into the shadows, Boots called out work assignments, adding, "Keep the shop secured. It's early, but better safe than sorry." She did not look back at Jack until the sound of air drills and other shop noises began.

She looked overhead and then said, mockingly, "I don't suppose I could induce you into going into my office?"

He shook his head no. Bootsie shrugged, an erotic gesture with movement all its own, pulled up an unidentifiable piece of scrap and sat down. "Then let's talk. What do you want out of me?"

"I want to be passed along, down the chain—to a base where I can do some good."

She pulled a drugstick out of her sleeve, and lit it, inhaling deeply. Its incense fragrance drifted toward Jack. Finally, she said, "That may not be in your best interests. As far as duplicating the suit goes, I have a lot of resources right here."

"It wouldn't take much for Pepys to put you out of commission—and once the suits are made, I need to train wearers. You won't be able to keep a secret here."

Gus stood by, cradling his rifle in the crook of his arm. "He's right about that, Boots."

Without diverting her gaze from Jack, she said, "Shut up." She tapped the ash from her stick.

"This isn't the only Skagboots' facility. I have one in the . . . country."

Jack answered, "Did you know lying adds years to your face?"

She frowned briefly and interrupted the expression by taking another deep draw on the drugstick. Finally, she said, "Who are you, anyway? And how did you get the armor?"

"I'm a Knight, or was, and how I got the armor follows. My name isn't important and I don't intend to give it to you any more than I intend to give you the suit. I don't wear an implanted ident chip and if you think to pull me down and take the suit anyway, be aware that it's fully powered and the deadman switch is in operation."

"You're definitely no virgin." Blue-gray smoke curled out of her pouty lips. "Damn that switch."

"It is an inconvenience." In actuality, Jack had all but permanently decommissioned the deadman circuit, knowing that Bogie could take the suit out of traitorous hands be they human or Thrakian. He didn't want to risk blowing up the armor if he could help it.

Boots crossed her legs, a stance that somehow cantilevered her breasts still further out of her jumpsuit. She gave him a measuring look before saying, "I don't know if I can pass you along the line that far. If you've been looking for us at all, you already know that we operate in three-person cells. Only one of those three knows anyone in another cell and so on down the chain."

He nodded.

She got to her feet, the swelling in her bosom fell victim to gravity, and Gus came to alert.

"Show him around, Gus," she ordered, "while I put a call through." She grabbed a metal cable and ascended the line like a trapeze artist, hanging by a loop about her wrist. Jack watched her in faint admiration.

Gus poked him in the ribs. "Follow me."

"Only as far as the hand truck can make it," Jack told him. The rifleman nodded.

The shop was a compendium of any shop Jack had ever been in. Degreasing vats next to lube pits, cubicles with workbenches clear or workbenches cluttered, according to the habits of the mechanic, hoists and overhead racks as well as the massive cherry pickers hanging from the massive framework of the building, the air pungent with the smell of solder. The degaussers were vintage, but the probes on the electronics benches were the finest technology out of the market. The later, he reflected, were probably stolen. There was a network of parts running through at a slow but constant pace, baskets swinging alluringly with their contents at eye level. Jack dipped a hand into one and came up with a couple of chips the size of his fingertip. He read the parts code and an eyebrow went up.

Gus laughed. "We got everything, boss," he said. His actual voice and tone was a physical echo of Bogie's, and made Jack smile. He made as if to drop the chips back, but Gus waved. "Keep 'em. You might need 'em someday."

Jack doubted he'd ever have to repair a laser cannon, but sealed the chips in an upper pocket.

The floor space became more and more crowded until Jack became aware that the hand truck could no longer follow. He stopped and Gus turned around, puzzled. "This is as far as I go."

The rifleman gave a nod, saying, "We got a lot of equipment stacked around." They retraced their journey to where they had begun, the hand truck hovers whining as if in protest over the unnecessary trip. Jack leaned down, reset the controls and let it settle.

Bootsie came down the cable as spectacularly as she had ascended, a slight frown marring her white-blonde beauty. "I've got my man on the line," she said. "And I'm to see the suit out of the box."

Jack had expected as much. He opened the lid as Boots summoned a portable cherry picker. He attached the hoist and let it draw Bogie to his feet. He held the helmet as the Flexalinks came to its full height. The Shop boss sucked in her breath admiringly.

She spoke to her handset. "I'd say he has the real thing." She read the reply and her glance flicked to Jack. "All right," she answered, closed the handset and clipped it on her belt.

She was in the process of saying, "You're cleared—" when all hell broke loose.

The air rumbled overhead, thunder low and mean, and Jack pulled Bogie down off the cherry picker as the building shook. Gus yelled, "Jesus, it's a strafing run!" and took off, rifle in hand as the boom, boom, boom of the shelling rattled the shielded warehouse. It was obvious the shields wouldn't take much more of a pounding.

Bootsie disappeared down a trap door previously obliterated by dirt and scrap. If anyone noticed that Jack did not need the hoist to hold the suit up on its own, they said nothing. He peeled open the seam, cursing Pepys. If he had to shoot the damn place down himself, he wasn't going to take any more.

Bogie crouched against his shoulder blade, lift functions a nearly imperceptible purr in his ear as he settled himself in the armor. He normally did not wear boots inside the armor boots, but now he had no choice. He tore his jumpsuit open from neck to waist, baring his chest to clip the leads on. This would be a messy suit-up, but time was of the essence. He seamed up. His wrists tingled, telling him his gauntlets were powered up and ready. As he bent to reach for the helmet, there was a screaming boom above, answered by a rending of metal, and smoke and fire poured in through the torn roof. One of the massive hoists tore lose from its track and dropped ponderously to the floor where scrap and machinery collapsed under its weight.

Through the roof, sky and smoke streams showed. He jammed his helmet on and looked up, even as the Talon's shadow began to dapple the skyline, the sun behind it, casting the darkness of betrayal ahead. Jack had target probability locked on before the strafing fire began again, and he fired his own wrist rockets into the hellish miasma whirling overhead.

The entire building creaked as the Skagboots' own crew answered the Talon's fire as well. The shadow fled amidst flame and laser scoring, but the helmet tracking told him that two more attackers were approaching. He targeted the best window for placing a hit. It was not likely his weaponry could bring down both planes, but they were overconfident and coming in far too low. He could do some heavy damage.

The helmet told him his targets were locked on as he raised his guantlets to the correct trajectory. "Help me hold it steady," he told Bogie, and the sentience locked his armor into position.

Sweat began to trickle down his forehead. Then the helmet released his wrist rockets, and he was shoved back on his boot heels by the force of the release.

Metal screeched. Air exploded. Water flamed. A cascade of smoke and fire poured earthward. Jack had only a brief instant to realize the overhead roof, what was left of it, was coming down on top of him.

The suit had taken worse, but not much, and his helmet was not screwed into place. As the machinery came down, sweeping by, catching him in a comet tail of cable and track, he lost his footing and his head.

Chapter 12

Amber hugged the shadowed ruined walls closely, her breath a whisper to her own hearing, her heart a pacemaker that the close-circuited security scanning must surely pick up. But she sensed no alarms and with a final step or two, knew she had breached the cordon about the bombed out wing. Her fingertips went to the choke collar about her slender neck and brushed the microcircuitry entwined there as if in thanks for its part in keeping her safe from detection. Pepys and his World Police were the height of security, but the black market managed to stay just one step ahead of them. And Amber never bought anything retail if she didn't have to.

Though the bombing had been blamed on the Green Shirts, she had thought for several months that the location had been more than coincidence. There had been no effort to either repair or raze the damaged section, almost as though Pepys were afraid to touch it. The Lunaii wing had housed the late Commander Winton's operation . . . some of it under the zegis of Pepys and some not, for the man who'd helped Pepys betray the Dominion Knights on Milos had had machinations of his own. Perhaps he had even aspired to replace the man he'd helped become emperor. As she eased farther into the pattern of broken shadows and shattered walls, she felt a tingle of ice down her back and halted.

With every sense she had left, she probed the area about her, and fought to stay hidden in this night that was death-dark.

Her thoughts briefly winged those of the psychics Pepys kept chained to his patronage in another wing; even they were unaware of her, and stayed so. Smiling ironically, she decided her sense of impending disaster was overdeveloped —and the longer she lingered in the ruins, the more likely she was to be found.

She slipped a pair of glasses down, and the black night instantly faded to gray. Confident, she moved toward a passageway and down it as though she herself were a ghost.

The console room had been blown from within like an eggshell. She ran a hand over a jagged plastic relic, its edges as sharp as tempered metal. There was little enough left of the room to identify its purpose, but Amber saw the melted lumps where plugs and leads had been, and barely recognizable shards of electronic equipment. Her nose curled at the still-rank odor of smoke, melted plastic and metal, the fumes of electric fire, and more. Winton, if he had lived, would probably have died in this room. It gave her satisfaction to know that Jack had, at least, been able to kill the man who'd hunted him. But as they'd both come to know, as despicable as Winton had been, he was no more than a hound to the man who'd controlled him.

And that man was Pepys.

Amber left the com room. Winton had been a deeply deceptive man. Wherever he kept his access terminal to his own computer files, it would not have been in the com room.

As she made her way down the crumbling corridor, she noted that the main structure of the wing was basically intact. The third story above her was gone, devastated by the main bank of blasts, but this second story was sound and the first story virtually unharmed except for the electrical fire that had swept through, and the smoke and chemical-dampener damage.

She passed a virtually untouched portal door and paused, in spite of the insignia showing it to be a janitorial area. Amber impatiently pushed her glasses up on her forehead and ran her fingertips over the door's seal. Faint blue sparks marked her intrusion. She jerked her hand back as though shocked. Her body flinch brought the glasses back down across the bridge of her nose where they landed smartly. She blinked at the abrupt change from darkness to twilight.

She put her hand out and touched the portal seal again. The glasses showed no sparking, but she felt as though she had touched something— slimy. Amber wiped her hands on the thigh of her pitch-black pants leg. Then, gathering her wits, she bent down to see what needed to be done to unlock the door.

The lock was simple and yet complex. A sound lock, with a retinal pattern for final release. She'd anticipated that and had brought along a holo-gram projector with Winton's pattern on it. The sound lock though—could be anything. And yet, as she stood, she smiled.

Why would such a locking system be on a janitorial door?

She looked back down the corridor. Close enough to the com room to be convenient—anyone seeing Winton about his daily business in this area would assume he'd be en route to the com room, especially if they knew him well. That included Pepys' spies within the palace as well as any outside spies. Before Winton's death and the bombing, the com room had been secret, se-cret enough to hide the real center of Winton's power.

All she had to do was break the lock to find out if she was right.

All she had to do was stand in the corridor and make the right sound to begin the unlocking se-quence. The right sound out of all the thousands upon thousands of sounds a human could make or command to be made.

She could eliminate a number of them. What-ever noise Winton would make in this passage-way to gain entrance, he would want it to be swift and inconspicuous. And, it would probably not have to be in his own voice, in case a subordi-nate needed to get in as well. A sound or noise anyone could make.

She canted her head, smiling wryly to herself, as she narrowed the field down from thousands and thousands to merely hundreds. Just in case she could get that far, she pulled the palm-sized projector out of a side pocket and affixed it over the lens plate for the retinal identification.

The man who had hunted her and Jack for years had been an impatient, snap-judgment personality, intensely shrewd and private. Knowing all of which gave her no clue as to the sound lock.

She could try to pull the lock out, like pulling the ignition from a hovercar, but it was likely the room was booby-trapped, like a deadman switch on armor.

From another pocket, she pulled another small piece of equipment, thumbed it on, and placed it over the lock. The tiny screen flat-lined, showing her no movement within the locking mechanism.

"Not yet," she muttered, as she checked the hologram's alignment. She laid her cheek against the cool door, thinking of the sound or word that might be the key.

Then, with a smile, she straightened and said the most unlikely word she could think of that would ever be heard within these walls.

The screen began to dance with life and as the retinal plate came on, and took a reading from the hologram projector, it spiked into frantic activity.

The door slid open quietly. Amber moved within its shadow among the shadows, snapping her equipment loose from the door before its slide into the frame could dislodge some very expensive equipment. She secured it among her pockets and brought her glasses into place once again before she moved into a room that was clearly not a janitorial locker.

The terminal equipment set up was sophisticated and functional. With a smile she sat down in the com chair. Now the real work began. She leaned forward to test her ability to access Winton's most private files.

She left in failure, knowing only that someone else, from another terminal, had a program running break-in possibilities for a tie-in as well. She could only guess that someone was either Pepys or Baadluster. To lift the program might give her more access, but it would also set off an alert. She had no choice but to make some inquiries among the people she knew, and return to try again. And again, until she either had what she wanted, or she'd been caught infiltrating.

As she passed through the cordons, she caught a flickering frame of thought and looked up, freezing to immobility. She knew that smoldering touch and searched the edge of the ruins, expecting to see Vandover Baadluster waiting for her.

But the thought curled away unexpectedly and she let her breath out.

Hugging her chilled hands to her ribs, she left the bombed out wing and made her sure way across the palace grounds. She knew where she was now and no one was her equal getting in and out of the grounds undetected. She wove her way in and out of security areas, dodging that smoldering flame of thought as much as she did camera eyes and heat scans. There was no quick way to do it. It was three steps here, a dart there, a painstaking pattern to be woven.

She nearly screamed when a heavy hand dropped

upon her shoulder from behind and spun her about. She shoved a first in her mouth to smother her noise and looked up, up at the burly phantom confronting her.

Before she identified him visually, her nose told her who it was. K'rok, Milot commander of the Knights, puppet commander of the Thrakian League. The musky scent of the ursine beastlike being invaded her senses and she blinked away a watering tear.

"Thought I had a thief, I did," K'rok rumbled. He dropped his pawlike hand from her shoulder. "What be you doing here, Lady Amber?" Faint illumination from beyond the barracks picked up a glimmer in his eyes as he stared down at her.

Before she could find a probable answer, he took a step closer and she felt enveloped by his presence as if he'd embraced her.

"It is not safe, friend of Storm. They be looking for you."

"I know," she got out, her voice thin and strained.

The Milot sniffed. She knew as if it was a certainty that he could smell the smoke and destruction on her clothing and in her hair. He rocked back a half step. "What be you doing in the Lunaii wing?"

"Let me go, commander." She shifted her weight imperceptibly to the balls of her feet, preparing to run.

He shook his massive head. "Not yet. I be thinking a while." And he stood in silence, as if that was just what he was doing.

Amber had nothing on her that would bring

down a Milot, nothing she had access to any longer, and she felt a desperate sense of loss over the psychic powers she had once had. Even of those powers she had once tried with K'rok and which his alien thick-headedness had turned away.

The Milot put his hand out suddenly, gripping her shoulder again. His voice lowered. "I feel in my heart that Jack is not dead. Knowing this, I feel also you must be doing work for him." With a sigh, the Milot lifted his head and she sensed that he looked in back of her, toward Pepys' palace. "I wish you luck," the being finished. "You must be careful. I am not trusted here by any being and cannot be helping you, except with well wishes." He turned her about, giving her an encouraging push toward the forest that edged the grounds and marked the final boundary of her freedom. "Good hunting," he said as she took to her heels, heartbeat thudding in her ears.

Chapter 13

The ache in his throat and lungs brought him awake. With every breath he took, it felt as though he'd been burned, the air rasping through seared tissue. He coughed, gasped with the pain, coughed again, and writhed with the effort except that he was pinned down and could do nothing more than toss his head. His eyes watered so heavily that he could not see, and he could not free his hands to wipe them.

It was somewhere in the middle of this misery that he realized he was still alive and that it was the suit which kept him so.

Jack wrinkled his brow and eyelids tightly, trying to wring his eyes dry enough to see. When he opened them finally, he got a hazy view of smoke and flame, of metal still hot enough to glow in the dark, and of a jagged portal to the evening sky. He heard low moans and cries. Plastic fumes stank on the raw air. He ducked his chin, found the drinking nipple operative and took a tiny sip of water. It stung all the way down, but the second swallow was easier.

He lay back, cradled in the armor, and concentrated on feeling his body, every contortion and ache, though in the gloaming he could see nothing below his neck. Half the building must have fallen on him. His feet felt numb until he realized it was the double booting constricting him. The realization halted the panicky drum of his pulse—he had thought he'd been crushed from the knees down.

His helmet was gone, torn away. It must lie beyond him, out of view and reach—and, he hoped, unnoticed by the scavengers which were probably already crawling all over the shop. Even as he began to assess his options, he could hear grunts and rattles, and a piece of sheet metal falling away, to crash on the flooring to his left. The noise echoed in his pounding skull. Jack closed his eyes tightly and prayed for the pain to go away so that he could think clearly.

Boss. . . . Bogie's voice, faded to a thready reflection of his normal hardy tones.

Jack realized that the comforting softness he pillowed his sore neck and head upon was Bogie. "Are you hurt?"

No. Hungry. . . .

The sentience was growing rapidly now, and his regeneration took all the sunlight he could absorb. Usually, through the suit and the built-in solars, it was no problem. But having been locked up, Bogie must be feeling drained. Though sunlight was his preferred energy source, Bogie could—and had—taken from Jack. How hungry was the alien?

Jack felt a cold sweat bead up on his forehead. "How bad is it?"

He sensed a peevish echo as Bogie only answered, *Hungry.*

His stomach clenched at the thought. "Me, too, Boog." With the helmet gone, he could not see his readouts. "Are we powered up or do we have a red field?"

Being buried would not drain the armor, but damage and shortage might. Although he did not smell the acrid scent of burned out circuitry within the suit, the air was full of it. There was no answer. Hair tickled the back of Jack's neck—was it sweat trickling down or was Bogie moving imperceptibly there? He had a sense suddenly of just how close and how warm the pulsing of his blood through his jugular veins might be.

Time to see how much power remained in the suit. He flexed his arm, felt weight shift about him, then slide away unstably. He quieted as he heard someone scrambling through the dark. Abruptly, to the far side of the shop, an arc light came on. Its blinding white light made the shadows darker on Jack's side of the destruction. It brought out, in sharp silhouette, two men crouched about five yards away from him, and ten meters up.

"I tell you I saw him put the armor on—"

"If he's dead then, so much the better."

Warningly, "Boots will want 'em in one piece."

The pile of debris shifted with an alarming noise. Bits of dust and particles sifted through the air, caressing Jack's face. He spat to one side and blinked painfully to keep his vision clear.

His right leg cramped as he tried to flex the armor. He made a noise through gritted teeth as his calf tightened and his leg convulsed in reaction, and missed part of what the gravel-voiced man said to his partner, the one with an accent he couldn't identify. Whatever it was they said, he could tell from the tone of voice it mattered little at this point what the shop boss wanted.

". . . get a light over here."

"Shut up and keep looking. He was close to the front door." A beam cut the air, not an arm's length from Jack's nose. "That's all that's left of the fracking front door."

A splintering rip, and a yell, and the light beam disappeared with a wild thrashing. The mountain of scrap groaned and swayed and Jack could hear large pieces breaking off and crashing to the floor. A pressure lifted off Jack's legs, one he hadn't known was there, but before he could drag himself free, the load shifted and he felt it settle down once more.

"Reyes! Where are you?"

A curse, and a moan. "Lost the fracking torch! Damn near got swallowed up. Give me a hand."

From across the shop, he could hear a shout, "Get me a block and tackle over here!"

The two men, intent on their own salvation, moved together, ignoring the command from elsewhere. Jack ground his teeth and concentrated on flexing his legs, carefully, without bringing down an avalanche.

"Where's the torch?"

The accented voice: "Frack the torch. You fish for it. Some of this scrap is sharp enough to take your arm off. Let's find the suit and get out of here."

"Suppose it's buried under this crap?"

Scornfully. "Then I suggest we start digging!"

There was a sliding noise, followed by the thud of feet hitting the floor not four paces from where he lay. "Here! I'll hand you down. Damn that arc light . . . this is like working on the dark side of a moon."

The voice Jack had come to identify as Reyes said, "I think I hear Quincy moaning . . ."

"Forget that ape! You're in with me and don't forget it."

"Yeah, but—suppose he's the one they need the block and tackle for. Maybe he's under something."

There was a scuffle. Breathing heavily, the gravel-throated speaker said, "You threw in with me, and don't forget it. I want that suit!"

"But Casper—Boots is only gonna split with you."

"Forget Boots! I've got my own scrap deal working and there's more money in it than you'll ever see if you stay with Skagboots'."

A sharp intake of breath, and another slight scuffle. The lighter, younger voice of Reyes made a breathy agreement, and then Jack heard footsteps moving in his direction.

There was another sound, a light scramble toward him, from another direction. Jack turned his chin toward it, unable to distinguish whether it was the debris shifting again or if something moved with purpose. Whatever it was, it was on a collision course with him and the two salvagers.

Light filled his eyes. He jerked his head back from the palm-sized beam, a small but handy tool he'd seen Amber use before.

"Shit! He's still alive."

"Then slice his throat and pull him out of there."

"Casper, he's got a small mountain on him. We ain't getting either him or the suit out easy."

A third voice, light and easy. "Actually, you're not getting him at all."

Jack blinked, squinting, unable to see forms other than as harsh black and white silhouettes. Two of them met with a clash. He smelled the warm scent of blood as something splattered his face.

The second man, his voice fairly dancing with pain, yelled, "Shit, I'm cut, I'm cut!"

There was a hiss of breath. "Back off! We saw him first."

The light and easy voice, a cavalier tone Jack almost knew. . . ."Ah, but possession is what counts, isn't it? And I found him first. That's a nasty cut. Perhaps you should concentrate on getting that taken care of?"

The rumbling voice Jack had tagged as Casper answered, "We're going. But we'll be back."

The cavalier man answered, "I don't doubt that. Your friend looks a bit pale . . . he's lost a lot of blood. You'd better hurry."

There was a lot of shuffling as the two men helped each other out the wreckage of Skagboots' front door.

A mellowed light beam switched on, as the third man illuminated both himself and Jack and bent down.

"I think we'd better see how we can get you out of here."

The face wasn't human.

Chapter 14

"It pleases me that the rumors of your death have been greatly exaggerated," the muzzled and sable-furred face said, with humor. "Although you seem to be in some trouble. I do, however, remember the time you dropped an entire dam upon yourself. Is this some obscure human death wish?"

The familiar tone was nearly washed out by the smell of fish. Jack recovered and said to the Fisher, "Are you going to get me out of here, or wait for someone else to come by to carve up?"

Skal's wolfish grin increased. "Perhaps that astonishing woman. There is something about her that stirs even my Fisher blood, though I doubt that sex between her and me would be possible or even desirable. No, great warrior, I am here to pull your fish out of the fire. I've been looking for you."

"How? How did you find me?"

The otter-man gave a rippling shrug. "Mist-off-the-waters sent me. She told the Elders the story of your death was untrue, and sent me . . . with this." In the moon-pool of light, the Fisher showed a bloody handknife in his palm, and Jack recognized the twin to a knife he had been given years ago.

Jack swallowed tightly. "That was a time ago," he said. Kavin, his mercenary friend and commander, had been alive then. So had the treacherous head of secret police, Winton. And Amber had been just a streetwise girl for whom his love could not be expressed.

"Water under the bridge," Skal returned and gave a barking laugh. "Now we must get you out of here!"

"I've got power enough to do it—but I was worried about getting reburied."

"I shall then mark the spot," Skal said. He stood, and the moon-pool of light moved with him. It shrank until Jack could no longer see it. Skal gave another laugh. "Jack! Your helmet!"

"Good. Secure it and stand clear."

The Fisher said wistfully, "I would be standing all the way home on Mistwald, if I could, my friend. Hurry."

Jack read the tone of his voice and knew that the Fisher mystic known as Mist-off-the-waters had not lightly sent Skal off-world into a society they scarcely knew. Skal had come to get him because they needed him.

Even as Jack tightened his muscles and prepared to use the suit to move, he knew he would have to put his own needs aside for the moment. The Flexalink answered his muscle command as it was meant to do, with the strength of hundreds, and the tons of scrap and debris shivered as the earth quaked below it.

* * *

"Money for passage is no problem," Skal told him over a mug of beer, and licked a few droplets of foam from his whiskers. "I have metal flake from our rivers that you people seem to value highly. It has its uses, I suppose, though it's too soft for metalworking other than jewelry."

Jack smiled at the Fisher's appraisal of gold. He'd seen Skal pay for the evening's round of drinks and food with a nugget. He set his mug down. "All the same, I'd keep that pouch of yours out of sight. Victor Three's a cesspool of cutthroats."

"Spoken by a man in a position to know." Skal took a deep draft of his drink, neck muscles rippling gracefully with every vigorous swallow. The otter-man seemed at home in the dingy, tacky bar.

"What sort of transportation do we want, then?" Jack hitched himself up gingerly in his chair. His stiffening muscles told him he'd be one massive bruise from head to toe come morning. A dented tool chest of considerable size rested next to his chair, and he put a boot foot upon it.

"I want the best and swiftest ship to Mistwald." Skal's laughing face sobered, merely by the lowering of his brows and flattening of his whiskers. "There's no time to waste."

"At least two weeks, with acceleration and decel—and that's if you have a Corsair or Talon. It's not likely we can get military transportation—" not to mention, undesirable to Jack in his present situation, but there was no need for Skal to know that, "—so we may have some waiting around. Who goes in and out of your sector?"

"No one but traders—and the despoilers."

"Traders take their time, it's less expensive that way, especially if they're hauling barges. And despoilers sound real difficult to buy passage from."

Skal blinked slowly. "You make fun of me, Jack."

"No. Not really. Who are these guys and what's the problem?" He paused to take a fresh bottle of beer from the little servo wheeling about their table and Skal did the same. "I know it's important or you wouldn't have come off-world looking for me."

"If we knew who they were, we would know how to pull their leashes—who to complain to in order to get them off, but we do not. The few spies we've sent after them have been sent back— dead. Very messily dead." Skal paused. His eyes glistened. "They have burned a wound into the land that cannot be healed. Their base is small, but growing, and we do not know if it is our world they want—if so, how could they treat it so carelessly?—or if they are using us as a stepping stone."

Despite the warmth of hot food and pleasant brew, Jack felt a chill. "Not . . ." he leaned forward, "not Thraks."

"No. This much I do know—they appear to be men such as you. Or alike to these Fisher eyes."

"Has the Council tried raining them away?" Jack remembered his days on Mistwald and the remarkable powers of the Elders with the weather.

Skal nodded. "Useless. They simply move to higher ground, and the stain of their existence spreads. An ulcerating sore along the riverlands. My own people can do nothing but send for you."

That must mean the Fishers were in an incredible bind. Jack had fought alongside Skal during their civil wars. The otter-folk had considerable ingenuity and courage. Or perhaps it meant only that anything off-world daunted them. They'd had a look at Jack's armor and knew the destructive power, far beyond their own, it held. They were brave, not foolish.

"Get me there," he said, "and I'll see what I can do."

Skal looked at him over the brim of his mug. "But," he answered, "I interrupted you on a quest of your own."

"It can wait."

Eyes that were much more than animal and yet different from his own looked at him closely. Then Skal said, "I bow to your wisdom, and thank you for your decision."

Jack picked up his mug. "Drink up. Port's open in the morning and we can see what's available then. In the meantime, I want to be drunk enough to sleep well—tomorrow's going to hurt."

Skal gave that barking laugh, his whiskers flared forward, and he met Jack's mug with his. "I hear you!"

They found an ambassadorial flagship from the Dominion that was willing to take on passengers. Jack had been in Dominion territory only twice in his life—both times to appear in Congress, but he had learned from Amber that people were slow to recognize other people; they saw what they expected to see. In Skal and Jack, the ambassador's aide and pilot saw an alien with an indentured mechanic, neither of any particular interest, but with enough gold flake to pay the berthing bills.

"Thus," observed Skal, "one hand scratches the other's back."

"Something like that," Jack answered. "And neither of us have to go into cold sleep." The flagship was nearly as fast as a military vessel, and he'd been asked to do some minor shop repairs instead of chilling down to save food and energy. Because of Skal's somewhat dubious physique, cold sleep had been bypassed altogether for him. The ship was well taken care of. Neither Jack nor Skal would be worked hard. If anything, the trip promised to be boring. Skal filled in the time making maps for Jack of the terrain around "the wound" and they discussed the various methods of approaching and observing without suffering the same fate as previous spies.

Skal twitched his sleek tail. "As if," he mumbled, "they had not been men!"

"Skinned?"

"Yes," the otter-man admitted, with a note of surprise.

Jack rubbed his four-fingered right hand absently. The Fishers had beautiful pelts—he would not put it past these freebooters, whoever they were, to go after those pelts. The thought made a hard, sour ball in his gut that bothered him for nights afterward.

*　　*　　*

Having his usual trouble sleeping, he finally got up one night and hauled Bogie's trunk down to the solarium. There, he shielded his eyes with a visor helmet and opened Bogie's case to all the glory of the nearest sun and let him bask in the energy. For his ears only, the alien sang a song of bloodthirsty happiness, warrior spirit that Bogie was.

Skal found him there, hand resting on the edge of the trunk much as if he had paused in rocking a cradle. He said nothing, but got a helmet to protect his own eyes from bedazzlement and sat down close to Jack. "We have been warned that we'll be entering warp speed by the beginning of next shift."

Jack nodded his understanding. The solarium would be closed down then—there being no sunlight in FTL. He sat, thinking that his journey was nearly half over, and Skal merely watched the greenness of the garden area, no doubt also thinking of home.

Then, after a long quiet, he said, "You have found that which lives in your armor."

"Yes."

"Mist told me of it, not long after you left us. She says it is a spirit being made flesh, like a cub in a womb."

"I think so." Jack took his hand from the lip of the trunk. "But what it is, I don't know."

"It's not one of you?"

Storm shook his head. "No. Nor one of anything I've ever met. It was given to me on Milos."

"I heard of that world . . . a sand planet now, is it not?"

"Yes."

Skal's tail flung angrily from side to side and he stilled it with great effort. "I did not mean to interrupt," he added.

"You didn't. I fought on Milos, a long time ago. The Milots didn't have a lot of faith we would ... beat the Thraks. They have great saurians there, berserker lizards, big murderous beasts, and they decided that the berserkers might be able to finish the Thraks off better than the infantry. They seeded our armor with the parasites. We didn't even know they were with us until too late. First they'd infiltrate our systems and then devour us. And when grown, they burst out of our suits like they were some kind of womb or egg-sac and they were really something to see." Jack paused, his mind filled with the horror of watching a berserker burst forth from what had once been a fighting comrade. "Berserkers are mindless fighters ... killing machines ... but even they couldn't save Milos for the Milots."

"And you thought your spirit was one such."

"Yes. And he may be akin to them. I don't know how much longer I can wear my armor. Right now he drinks light. Later, things may be different."

Skal sat back. "And yet this relationship is not all one-sided. I sense he helps you in many ways."

"Oh, yes. He can take over some of the minor suit functions. He has a mind of his own ... I can hear him, sometimes. He lends me his warrior spirit when I need it."

Skal pulled his muzzle apart in a smile. "One

hand scratches another back. May you and I share such helpful companionship."

Jack laughed at the Fisher's favorite fractured saying, pulled out of his reverie once and for all, and did what his friend obviously desired. The otter-man sank into blissful grunts all the while directing the scratcher. "A little higher there—just under the shoulder blade. No . . . now down. Aaaah."

The flagship came screaming out of warp drive, torquing into decel in the maneuver known as "turning the corner." The gravity of the movement pinioned Jack to his cot as if he'd been nailed there, his stomach somewhere about his sternum. Missing decel was about the only advantage he could think of to cold sleep. It was not enough of an advantage to make him use it any more than absolutely necessary.

Skal gave off a groan from the far hammock.

"Hang on," Jack told him.

"I should not have had that last beer for lunch."

"This is no place to be sick. Did your mother whelp a stomachless cub?"

"Ah, Jack," the Fisher moaned. "We've been together too long. Now you talk like I do."

"I won't be worried until I *eat* like you do." Jack lay back as the pressure moved to his forehead, to a spot between his eyebrows, and nailed him to the center of the universe. His stomach did a slow roll as it settled back where it belonged. His ears popped and he could feel the braking of the flagship.

Skal gave a noisy belch. The stench of stale

beer flooded the cabin. It did not bode well for either of them.

"Hang on," Jack repeated. "Think of home."

"Yesss," said Skal. "Home . . . only days away."

Home. Skal touched Jack on the forearm, motioning him to the hover. It was not raining over this flatland of Mistwald, not far from the lands he and Amber had so lightly called Swampberg, but the air was heavily dewed. Bogie was self-motivating behind him, and the armor lumbered to a halt. They were going to Council, but Jack was armed, in Enduro bracers, his weapon rigged. Security at the port had been heavy—what Triad authorities were looking for, neither Jack nor Skal knew, but neither of them had come all this way to fail now. Skal's authority on his homeworld became obvious when neither of them had to pass customs, a quarantine, or a Triad sweeper.

"What is security for," the otter-man said philosophically, "if it works against you?" But he had taken care, nonetheless, getting Jack cross-continent and past the growing stilt-cities, including Swampberg.

The sun shimmered prismatically off the air as Skal said, "It will be raining soon."

Jack glanced across the gray clouds dappling the purpled mesas he remembered would be their destination. Though Skal had not summoned them, or told them he would be coming, they both knew the Council would be waiting for them. He was often sorry he had not brought Amber to them, for the mystic or psychic world was second nature to them, and they might have helped her with her own tortured powers if only Jack had thought of it. Instead, she had gone a more damaging way for help. He took a deep breath. The world was alive, verdantly so. It would be a damnable shame if either man or Thraks should ever ruin it.

He shook off his memories and thoughts of Amber as Skal straddled the hoverbike.

"Will that carry all three of us?"

"Maybe not," the other answered. "Would you rather walk? Or float upstream, perhaps?"

Though it was a four passenger bike, the armor's weight was more than equivalent to two. Jack motioned Bogie to mount the last seat, and he settled behind Skal. The hover whined irritatingly as the Flexalinked alien sat down, but it stayed afloat. "Not high," Skal said. "Or fast. But steady." His hand-paw squeezed the brake off and away they went.

They gained the last mountaintop with a great deal of difficulty, but Skal would not hear of putting Jack down and leaving him to follow after with the armor. His muzzle tightened and his whiskers went flat.

"They sent me after you," he said, "and I'll be fried before I'll come back empty-handed."

And so they walked in together, Jack ducking his head, their presence filling the massive cavern's entrance. Skal preceded him slightly, cupping something in his paw.

The Elders were all seated about a low-burning, sweet-smelling fire. A waft of the smoke stung Jack's eyes, but he saw Skal approach Mist-off-the-waters and drop a bloodied handknife into her palm.

It disappeared into a curl of smoke itself and she puffed it into the air.

The cream-colored otter-woman smiled, saying, "Welcome, Jack Storm. Sit and talk with us."

Jack told Bogie to stay by the cavern entrance, and then did as he had been bid.

Chapter 15

Minerals caught the glow of the fire and reflected it back from cavern walls, giving the impression of a thousand tiny stars caught in stone. Niches were filled with tallow candles, squat and low as he remembered them, as if they burned down but never out. Their light pearlized the armor standing on guard at the cavern's mouth. The reflection caught Jack's eye—for a moment he wondered as he knew what it felt like to see the armor for the first time. He had been mistaken for a messenger of a god before. Now he knew why.

Mist put her hand-paw on Jack's arm, drawing his attention. She said, "You know many of the Elders from before."

Jack nodded as the silver-muzzled Fisher opposite him in the circle scratched his rump with his one hand. "One-arm," Jack said. "And Little Fish who is now gracefully grown. Bald Top here has lost a little more fur, but looks well—"

The knobby russet-furred otter-man blinked large, wet eyes and looked at him without a word.

"And Mist, of course. And I remember two or

three more of you, though I was never given your names beyond that of Elder."

Bald Top gave a grunt then, saying, "Well met, Little Sun."

The nickname made Jack flush. He felt his skin grow warm, and he wondered what sport the Fishers made of him this time, as well as last, for he did not understand his name. He settled for, "Well met," in answer.

Skal reported, "It took nearly all of the metal flake to bring him here."

One-arm waved his still raven-black arm. His body was silver-tipped with age, but where his pelt stayed dark, not a single light hair marred it. "No matter, Skal. It served its purpose. You were long, but not as long as we feared. As Mist has explained off-world to us, you could have been lost forever among the stars."

"I would have come back, no matter what."

Little Fish spoke up, "We know." She brushed her whiskers back with the palm of her hand, as Skal did, and continued a bit farther along her scar tissue.

Mist had not taken her hand off Jack's wrist. Now she squeezed a little as she said, "We apologize for taking you away from your business. We understand that you are sacrificing for us."

"It's no sacrifice, Mist. I wasn't having much luck finding what I was looking for, anyway." With Skagboots' destroyed, he'd lost his trail for the moment. "Tell me what's been happening here? Have you found any patches of rusty dirt, sand that is not normal?"

The Elders looked at him without answering.

"Can you try describing the ships they're using?" Briefly, Jack sketched out what a Thrakian warship looked like.

Bald Top lifted a gum, showing teeth only slightly worn by age. "Man, we know only that they use airships—we cannot help you there."

Frustrated, Jack shook off Mist's hold. "I can't help you blindly," he said. "I can't fight an army, no matter how powerful you think that suit is."

One-arm said, mildly, "We saw you melt a mountain with it last time."

"That wasn't a mountain, it was a boulder—you all saw it—" He looked about the circle and saw sleekly furred faces devoid of any expression he knew how to read. He began again, ended up muttering, "Damnit."

Little Fish said bitterly, "Do not despair. Ours is the despair. The land, poisoned. The river, a bitter drink of death . . ."

"How? Just tell me how."

She blinked. "If we knew how, Little Sun, we would not have needed you."

He sat cross-legged. He dropped his hand under his knee and clenched it. "Tell me what is happening. Skal calls it a wound, a canker that will not heal. Don't smoke the sweet-smoke and give me your mystic farseeings. Tell me what's happening."

"Fish, dying. Cubs downriver, born with two heads."

"What?" Jack swiveled to look at the Elder otter-woman who'd finally spoken. She wore a leather apron and he recognized the avocation if not the Fisher—she was a miller. The chaff and husks of rin, a ricelike grain, dusted her apron. "Are you certain?" That sounded more like radiation leakage, but he'd never been on-planet at the start of a Thrakian invasion. Leakage from landing perhaps? Fishburg had been somewhat advanced, using breeder reactors for electrical energy. "Skal, is there a reactor in the area?"

"No . . . and our detox programs and filters are functioning well at the other operating stations. I thought of that, too, when the canker first began. But there is no doubt it came with the strangers."

"Have you tried setting up a filtration system on the river, just in case?"

"We cannot get close enough," One-arm snorted. He thumped his chest and released a belch. "They could be floating turds downstream for all we know."

Jack looked at Skal. He could find no motivation for freebooters to be doing anything the Fisher claimed was happening. "You could be wrong. They could be Thraks instead of men."

The Fisher lashed his tail. "You are worried about *sand*, then?"

He nodded.

Mist said, "These Thraks are old enemies of yours?"

"Very old. Sand—the type of sand they make for their eggs and larvae—is devastating. If it's started here, it must be stopped immediately. Or else there is no hope for Mistwald." The sand-making microcosm, once unleashed on a widespread basis, was virtually impossible to stop. He hoped desperately that was not the case here.

"Have you been to the ambassador here? Or your emperor—what's his name?"

"Shining fur-grinning tooth is in charge still, but he is embroiled in trading pacts. Up to his fat neck in "free samples." He has turned away from his people and you can expect no help or hindrance from him. As for others—one stranger is the same as another, eh?" And Skal shrugged. His dark fur undulated.

Jack heard the unsaid honor in Skal's voice. He alone was not "a stranger." He alone they had hoped would help them. He took a deep breath and looked across the cavern at Bogie. One man against a Thrakian base installation was a pretty tall order. He exhaled. "I think I'd better have a look at this 'wound' as soon as possible."

Mist protested, saying, "I must read the smoke for you first, Little Sun, and give blessing—"

He didn't want to know what his future was. He'd fight better without knowing. "It's better I not know," he told her.

Her eyes widened. They had appeared merely dark in the gloaming of the cavern, now he saw and remembered their midnight blue color. She sat back on her haunches at the implication of his words.

But another Elder took it as insult and jumped to his feet. He palmed the hilt of a wicked look-ing hunting knife sheathed at his belt. "I demand an apology," the Fisher snapped.

Skal held up his hand. "It is not necessary that Jack apologize. It is we who should apologize to him, for forcing our customs upon him."

"But he slurred Mist—"

"I'm sorry," Jack interrupted. "I did not mean to slight any of you. But there is much ahead of us, and many outcomes, and I would rather not have one vision blinding my sight."

Mist got up. "He speaks rightly. The smoke only tells what it wishes. Storm has come to help us, as we asked. I suggest we let him." Her ironic tone fell on the short, rounded ears of the folk.

The skimmer groaned as much as it had before. Skal navigated by the stars in a now clear sky, a sky that was as velvet blue as Mist-off-the-waters' eyes. "You might as well rest," he said to Jack, who pillowed the back of his head on his hands and watched overhead. "We've a night's travel."

"That far?"

"The other side of the continent."

"About as far away from the spaceport as it can get?"

Skal nodded. "If it were not for the trouble in our own remote outposts, we might never have discovered its presence until the wound was much greater.

A shudder moved through Jack. He covered it by sitting up. "I don't suppose you intend to fly in?"

The Fisher threw him a sharp-muzzled grin. "Of course not. We land downriver and circle inland."

"Across mud?"

"Not so lucky. 'We'll be in a fairly dense rain forest. You'll be able to keep your boots dry, but it might be a tight squeeze for those broad shoulders." Skal flipped a thumb back at the armor.

What a Fisher and what Jack considered dry footing were two different things. He settled down on the work skimmer seat moodily. A rain forest meant rain. Several times a day, if the season was right. And it was always rainy season on Mistwald.

He was glad Flexalink couldn't rust.

Jack and Skal finished tugging the skimmer into a branch lean-to for camouflage. Bogie provided most of the power to move the transport, but he was like an uneducated robot—he had the strength and absolutely no idea of what to do with it—completely without a clue as how to apply himself. Jack had shouted himself hoarse giving instructions until Skal looked at him and said, "Don't let him pull. Make him push." And they guided it in. The last pink-purple cloud of dawn faded before they were done.

As Jack tugged the last branch over, the Fisher looked at him, and his brows went up. "Why not wear the armor? You are a soldier and it is your equipment."

Jack pulled his pack out of the skimmer and began unpacking his Enduro bracers and weapons belts, both the waist and the shoulder belts. "Normally I would. But I'm going to be outnumbered anyway—this way there's two of me. Bogie is short on a lot of concepts, but he knows how to stand and fire."

Skal moved his gaze in Bogie's direction. "I

just wondered who chose the targets. I have a gun, but I would not trust it to aim itself."

Jack read the unease in the other's voice. He straightened and clipped the last bracer onto his left arm. "I cannot explain to you the way we work. We've not done it often this way, but we have done it. My enemies are his enemies." He checked his energy clips and threw the empty pack into the skimmer.

"All the same, I would guard my back if I were you," Skal said. "Perhaps he is tired of sharing the armor with you when he must." The Fisher brushed past him, hiking up the riverbank toward a fringe of heavy, dark foliage that seemed as tall as a small mountain—the edge of the rain forest.

With a sigh, Jack called out, "Follow me, Bogie."

"Yes, boss," the armor replied in its deep and mellifluous voice, utilizing a synthesizer inside the suit. "The sun feels good."

"Enjoy it while you can." Jack hiked his shoulder belt into a more comfortable position across his chest and set off after Skal, who was moving across a grassland through stalks up to his neck.

Skal had not warned him of the clouds of insects, the winged variety, though not of the kind that enjoyed bare skin. Still, he finally fashioned a veil across his face to avoid breathing in the small, translucent green ones, with wings of such delicacy he wondered how they could survive the rain. The insects flew in layers, until the topmost skimmed the height of the rain forest, fewer, but with wingspreads that equaled the reach of his arms, and each layer occasionally dipped downward to feast on lesser flyers. He had never seen such brilliant colors.

"Bogie, make sure the suit cameras are on. I'd like to tape this for Amber."

"Recorder on." The armor lumbered after him, with a sound of grass being ripped out by the roots as it tangled about the boots and Bogie walked on, oblivious.

Skal met them at the forest's edge. He tugged playfully at the lower edge of Jack's veil. "Now you know why I have whiskers."

"Is that why? I thought it was to strain the river for fish."

Skal broke out in his laugh, until his amber eyes streamed. He mopped them with the back of his hands and reached out to slap Jack on his shoulder. In quite a different voice, he said, "Two of our scouts met their death in this forest. Good hunting to you, my esteemed friend and foe, and take care." Skal stepped away and literally melted into the forest shadows, his sable fur with caramel mottles as good a camouflage as Jack had ever seen. If it were not for the bright yellow slicker shorts and weapons belt, he would be invisible.

Sombered by what Skal had said, Jack ducked his head under a branch and entered, hoping that he had enough firepower to not need invisibility.

The sun, if there was one, Jack thought, must be overhead. He could feel a kind of smoldering green heat filtering down toward him through the layers of insects which were only slightly

less dense than they had been over the grassland. Only here there were more predators ...
flutterers disappeared with regularity at the flick
of a sticky tongue, but Jack had yet to see what
caught them. He eyed overhanging branches fre-
quently, but the dimness of the forest made it
damn near impossible for him to get a clear look
at anything. The dry footing Skal had promised
was here, but he was sweating enough inside his
boots to float his ankle bracers off.

Behind him, the armor moved with surprising
delicacy as Bogie learned to negotiate a passage
through without tearing branches off to do so.
Skal's ears moved forward and back and he complained about noise, but the complaints and the
noise had both trailed off.

Jack called out, "Where are we?"

"Close to the other side."

Jack had no such feeling. If anything, he thought
they'd been going in circles. He said to Bogie,
"Check your compass."

The alien asked, "In reference to what?"

Damn. He'd not set an initial coordinate and
Bogie had nothing to draw the primary median
on for reference.

Skal had come to a stop and watched Jack over
the top of a bar of what looked (and smelled) like
dried fishmeal. "If you have a problem," he got
out, "take a sighting from above." His whiskers
trembled with humor.

Jack knew a dare when he heard one. He looked
up, selected a tree, and said to Bogie, "Give me a
leg up."

The armor stood motionless for a moment, then stood on one boot and ponderously held the other leg in the air.

Jack shook his head. "No, no. Give me a hand up."

Bogie righted himself on his feet and spread his gauntlets.

"No," Jack said. "Listen." And he thought an image to Bogie, of being given a boost.

Obediently, the armor bent and did so. As Jack shinnied to the limb above him, Skal said. "That's the dumbest robot I've ever seen."

Before Jack could say anything, Bogie reached over to Skal, picked him up by the Fisher's weapons' belt and neatly deposited him on the bottom branch.

"I'm learning," rumbled Bogie gently.

The otter-man hooked an arm about the tree trunk and said to Jack, "I think I'll just wait here for you."

Hiding his expression, Jack kept climbing.

The tree was a slender, fragrant growth, with a light brown skin that peeled down naturally to creamy white. He had to take care it did not peel away too vigorously under him, making handholds and footholds chancy. The branches were spaced wide apart at regular intervals, making it a natural for climbing. The scent of its bark was heady and Jack thought of Amber wearing its perfume. She'd like it.

Below, Skal made a hiss between his teeth, saying, "Watch where you put your hands, Jack my friend."

Distractedly, Jack looked at his right arm, extended for a pull up and saw the brown and cream lizard not a finger's length from his hand. The reptile's tongue wagged out, and then the beast turned about on the branch. A shambling run, a leap with all legs spread, the wattle on each catching the air, and it parasailed to a nearby branch.

"That one leaves a nasty bite, but it's also timid," Skal offered to the treetops.

"I'll remember that." Jack kept climbing.

As the tree broke the forest ceiling, the wind that the forest had shunted away took hold and swayed it, and Jack could only balance on a slender branch and embrace the main trunk. He marked the direction Skal had been taking—the Fisher's sense was leading them where he said it was.

His sweat dried quickly in the stiff breeze. As Jack half-turned to head back down, he saw a good-sized clearing in the rain forest—and his heart skipped a beat.

Rust! Nothing—where there should have been trees or at least grass, there was nothing but rusty dirt.

Sand. He could not be wrong.

Jack rubbed a free hand over his face, tired from the half-day's walk. He looked back toward the destination Skal guided them to—and saw a thin curl of smoke on the horizon.

Habitation of some sort. Yet the sand was here, in the forest.

Jack got down the quickest way he knew how, which was halfway between sliding and a controlled fall. Skal saw him coming and bailed out of the tree first with a startled yelp.

"Are you bit?"

"No." He reached for Bogie and unscrewed the helmet. "Computer, mark this location as a return target." He replaced the helmet, saying to Bogie, "The in-suit circuitry will mark that. Just follow the readings on the way back."

Bogie, who could not actually see but made his way by rightness and wrongness of various suit readings, answered, "Yes, boss."

Skal's whiskers were up, like hackles. "What is it?"

"There's an installation that way, over the ridge. We'll get an overview of it when we break clear of the forest. But I don't understand why because there's sand that way—" Jack thumbed the direction. "They don't leave the sand once they plant it. Usually they'll dig a below ground nest, infiltrate there, and then start the sand."

With a worried frown, the Fisher said, "We're going to see?"

"Yes."

Skal let him take the lead.

An hour later, bare head wet with perspiration, Jack knelt by the patch of Thrakian sand. Skal also knelt, his lips wrinkled with disgust.

"This *sand*—it's not natural."

"No. It'll ruin Mistwald, the way it did Milos and my world, Dorman's Stand, and a handful of others. But it's been abandoned here." Jack stood up slowly, and surveyed the damage. The patch was large, and he could see burn marks along the leading edge. And no Thraks. But why?

"All right, Bogie. Take us back to the return target."

The armor led them back. Skal and Jack sat down and took a short break. Skal had fishbars which Jack refused, but he also had a rich fruit and grain bar, one that had Jack licking his fingers when it was gone. They shared a waterskin and got up, ready to go on.

Mistwald's sun was penetrating the rain forest at about two o'clock high when they broke cover. The forest was elevated, and the grassy plains broke out from under them, rolling down to more knolls and a set of falls, three of them, boiling water into the air. At their edge, Jack saw the installation. Jack sucked in his breath in at the size of the runway being cut into the green field even as he watched, domes going up, a crude cutaway of dirt taking a bank of fire as a squad lined up before it. The air stank with the fumes and rang with the noise. The base was going to be massive—it would have to be to hold three launching cradles as well as three runways. He saw Talons and corsairs, their shapely and deadly bodies resting to one side.

"God in heaven," Jack said. "They're getting ready to start a war."

"Who?" Skal asked, digging at his arm. "Who!"

"The only ones brave enough to defy Pepys and go after *sand* themselves. Those are Green Shirts down there. That explains why the sand in the forest is dying back. They've already dug out an infestation."

The Fisher made a growling noise deep in his throat. "What good is medication," he said, "if it kills the patient?"

Jack stayed at the forest's edge, watching the base crawl with fighters. Once he went down there, there was no going back. And yet, how could he help Skal without going in?

Bogie moved. The helmet visor went up as if he were a hound scenting the wind. "I smell death," was all he said.

Chapter 16

The Fisher had no mane at the back of his sleek head, but his pelt was stiffened, hackles up. "I agree," he said. "Now that we know who the enemy is, we shall know how to defeat him."

Jack shook his head. "Create a diversion. I'm going down there."

"You're *what*?"

Storm dropped to one knee. He began untangling grasses and ferns from the armor's boots, unwilling to meet Skal's too bright eyes. "You knew I was in the Outward Bounds on a mission of my own. Mist knows it, too. I was looking for Green Shirts, Skal. Looking for a way to disentangle Pepys from his web of power—and looking for myself."

"They despoil my world."

Jack stopped, his hands stained by the vegetation he held across them. "I know. They're careless—heedless—of the damage they're bringing with them."

Skal's muzzle wrinkled and he spat viciously to one side, just missing Jack. "You think I'm not aware of your worlds just because I remain earthbound to mine? I listen to the news. I have seen the damage inflicted by your 'careless' heroes. They are terrorists."

Jack looked up and met his gaze, as bright and hot as magnesium in water. "You're right," he said, and got up, dusting his hands on his pants. "They're nothing more than murderers and bombers. But they could be more. I think they meant to be, once. And they have helped me, in their own selfish way, and I don't have anywhere else to go for the help I need now. They have my mind, Skal, memories they took when I slept as a soldier. I need those memories, and I need to remind them who they were. Then we can part ways."

"And what of Mistwald? When you are done here, and leave—what of them?"

"They helped you here. They fought sand when you didn't even know it was here. They've taken out a vital first step in Thrakian infestation. They've done more than you know."

The Fisher said bitterly, "They despoil the wilderness ... our forests and our water. They will kill us as surely as they did the Thraks— and without merciful quickness."

"Contact them. Tell them what they're doing. They may listen."

"If not?"

"It's them or the Thraks, Skal. You can put up filtration dams along the river and lakes—that'll solve a lot of the problems. Thraks ... Thraks won't stop unless they're forced to."

Skal smoothed the side of his muzzle, laying his whiskers back. "I gave you a knife once."

There was a lump in Jack's throat and he found it difficult to swallow around it. "I know."

"You know nothing! Not then, not now!" Skal paced away, his tail rigid with his agitation. "That knife signifies an honored enemy. It signifies a mercy kill, if the battle is lost. I trusted you, we trusted you, to quicken our death if we lost the battle for Mistwald. I came to know you as friend as well. But you intend to go down there and join them, do you not?"

Jack had his hand on the suit's shoulders, preparing to open up the seams. He did indeed intend to go down and see if he could breach the camp's perimeters. But he would do it in armor. He paused, "Skal, you don't understand."

"I understand enough! You have betrayed your emperor, and now you betray us."

His throat constricted further, but he got out, "I haven't betrayed you, but I don't intend to make them leave. Give me time to do what has to be done."

"You're not going to fight them."

"No."

Skal took a deep, quivering breath. Jack watched his large amber eyes, searching for the expression that would tell him his life was in danger, but he found only sadness.

The Fisher said, "What shall I tell the Council? What of our dead?"

"Tell the Council I am meeting with the men building an unauthorized base here, and that I will ask for reparations if the Council will grant them authority to stay. As for your dead ..."

Jack paused. "It's possible the Thraks killed them. I don't know."

"It's equally as possible your Green Shirts did."

"I know. Tell the Elders I apologize for the arrogance of the human race. Tell them we don't always recognize the worth of another. Tell them I will see that the families of the dead are given prime trading rights, as well as an apology."

"Do humans know how to apologize?"

Jack found himself nodding. "Yes. Yes, we do."

The Fisher's sable tail relaxed slowly until it trailed on the ground. "Then, my friend," Skal said joylessly, "I will go back alone and tell of your betrayal with good intentions. If they attack you as they did my brothers, I don't think you'll be easy to pull down in your armor. But if they do, I will be back to avenge you." He offered his hand in farewell.

Jack took it uneasily. His hearing caught a high sound, just out of range, but near enough to be audible and to jar across his nerves. Even as he took Skal's hand, and began shaking, he lifted his head and half-turned on one heel.

He saw a glint in the sky. The whining pitch became clearer. "Damn! Skal, run for it. Bury yourself as deep in the forest as you can get." He swung about on the suit, took the helmet off, and collapsed the armor by opening up the seams.

"What is it?"

"And I was wondering about getting past security!" Jack sat down and shed his boots and legs bracers as quickly as he could. "Those are needlers—Thrakian warships. They've come after the base. This whole area will be—poisoned—with their weaponry."

As quickly as he shed the Enduros, Skal put them on.

"You can't come with me." Jack panted in his haste, shucking himself of his armor and weapons belts.

"You cannot tell me, friend, that *they*," and Skal jacked a thumb skyward as the needlers came screaming closer, "will not target you once they have seen you."

No, Jack couldn't tell him that. This whole confrontation was beyond the Alliance, and the Thraks would react to his armor as if he were an ancient enemy and all that had ever gone between them was hatred and war.

The Fisher arched his brow triumphantly. "Someone must survive to take back your apology."

Jack shoved himself into the armor, hastily clipping on leads and feeds, checking the screens to make sure he was fully powered. Skal leaned in, nose first, and eyed the chamois that was Bogie's regenerating form.

"This is the other?"

"Yes."

"Interesting." Skal nearly lost a set of whiskers as Jack heaved the suit up over his shoulders and finished sealing the armor at his neckline.

"Check your weapons," Jack recommended as he flexed his gauntlets. "Bogie, take stun off, make all shots fully operational."

Yes, Boss.

The ground shook beneath them as the needlers' rumbling made the earth vibrate. As Jack screwed the helmet on, he watched the Green Shirts' base go to a scramble. Planes on the ground meant maximum vulnerability. Whatever they could get up after the pair of needlers made their first run and circled to come back could well be the firepower that saved their asses.

Jack checked his targeting grids and cameras. The Green Shirts had better thank whatever gods they acknowledged that this was first turf for the Thraks, or they'd be facing incoming missiles. The Thraks were limited to short-range and unbased weaponry until they felt they were strong enough to take the port with all its defenses and warning systems.

Thunder sounded. The needlers were coming in, and they'd be there long before he was close enough to do any damage himself. But he'd be there when they came in to finish the base off. He grabbed Skal by the back of the neck even as the Fisher was patting down his ammo clips, and broke into a run only the seven-league boots of the armor was capable of.

Colin moved away from the building's exterior monitors, a most uncharitable expression curdling his face. Those damn Thraks. Even the twilight could not hide their spindly presence. He was the same as imprisoned, and he knew it, and they knew he knew it and did not care. He clenched a fist. Then he caught a deep breath and opened his hand, forcing it to relax. At one time it had taken more than the sight of a few sentry Thraks ostensibly guarding the Walker headquarters to upset him. Now it was one more in a series of senseless, destructive acts.

Pepys had gone insane. Colin saw no other term for it. The emperor, in stretching out his authority to minor, fringe planets, was in relentless pursuit of power. As suspicious as the Walker prelate was of the Green Shirts, he saw more of the emperor's scheming behind the recent outbreak of petty infringements, infringements which by their nature made it necessary for the emperor and his Thrakian allies to step in and settle the problems. The Outward Bounds, while under the jurisdiction of neither the Triad Throne or the Dominion, was in danger of being annexed. Walker information filtering in to him told him the freer spirits of the Outward Bounds would not stand still for Pepys' actions, even if it meant full-scale war—a war Pepys could no more afford with the Ash-farel threatening him and with his dubious alliance with the Thraks than he could safely behead himself and hope to live.

Colin waited now for the latest intelligence from Denaro. Pepys had infiltrated his own com lines—his most reliable information came in person, shielded by white noise screening—but now Colin wondered if Denaro were still reliable. Nothing had ever been said about the Gibbon incident—yet the young man surely knew, by Colin's subtle change in reliance upon him, that he had been suspect.

A step sounded behind Colin now and he turned. Jonathan had let Denaro in with little fanfare. The man stood, his frame braced defiantly. There was the natural arrogance of the young in the tilt of his head. "What news?"

"Farseeing is gone, your eminence, under the aegis of the emperor, reportedly to defend it from the Ash-farel."

The words struck to his very marrow. He held himself erect, knowing that he was under scrutiny from one who hoped to replace, as well as inform, him. "Gone? What do you mean—gone?"

"Annexed. I didn't mean—the Ash-farel veered in their attack, and left the colony clear. But they had forsworn themselves as Walkers by then, and begged for Pepys' protection."

"I see." Colin crossed his small private apartment, seeking the redwood table of old Earth, still finding solace in its burled rings of life and energy. "And were the Ash-farel indeed moving in for attack?"

Denaro brushed a hand through his untamable hair. "I can't find confirmation of it. It appears that agents infiltrated the ports first, sir, and after—readings can be altered, even falsified."

"Easily." Colin sat down, his palm on his table. "I cannot blame the colonists on Farseeing for being," and he gave an ironic smile, "shortsighted. Life is precious far from home. They did what they thought necessary."

"But your holiness—"

"Oh, damn me, Denaro. Stop treating me as if I were a fragile relic. I'm a flesh and blood man and no more holy than you are."

Denaro stepped back as though he'd been struck. He stammered for a reply and finally got out, "Sir."

"They had no more chance to stand against a staged attack than a real one. No, I don't blame them. Pepys orchestrated it well." Colin looked up, frowning. "You'd better instruct Jonathan and Margaret to contact the others and warn them of the tactic, though I doubt Pepys will try it twice."

"Yes, sir." Denaro's head bobbed. "But why now?"

"Now? Because now he is allied with the Thraks."

"But couldn't he have done the same when he was fighting them?"

"Maybe. But then, there was a good possibility the invasion would have been real. No. The Thraks are not holding off obtaining more crèche worlds because of the alliance. They are allied because they're less afraid of us than of the Ashfarel. They need us to buffer them. Fear is like an acid. The Thraks intend for it to eat through us first."

Denaro stood in silence while Colin thought a moment, then added, "What about the records?"

The young man's cheeks reddened in shame. "Nothing was destroyed. They thought—they thought an attack by the Ash-farel would take care of it. They never thought to destroy the . . . sensitive . . . material before Pepys took over."

The realization made Colin feel old. He took his hand from his table, the serenity he'd gathered washed away once more. The colony at Farseeing had been one of the biggest, most self-sufficient Walker outposts, and had been located at a crux between the Dominion planets and the

Outward Bounds, as the warp drives were navigated, rather like Bythia on the other axis. The information which had fallen to Pepys would do no overt harm but it would fuel Pepys' own insecurity and insanity.

The only empire Pepys feared was the empire he thought Colin was building. It had done no good to tell his old friend that it was God's empire, and there were no boundary lines.

He said to Denaro, "Watch your step. Pepys will build a case for treason if he can."

"Tr-treason?"

Colin let the corner of his mouth twist in a bitter smile. Denaro was a militarist Walker—meaning that he was not waiting for the meek to inherit any of the planets they touched. But now that he faced open conflict with the emperor, he was shocked and unready. Good. Colin did not want a pitched battle between Pepys and the Walkers. "Yes. Pepys has long feared that I might make a better ruler than he. He supplanted Regis, and has waited his whole life for that to happen to him. We must see that his wait is futile."

"I . . . see."

Colin watched the young man closely. If Denaro truly intended to wrest the Walkers away from him, he'd just handed Denaro his head on a platter. He would be living on borrowed time.

Colin sighed and got back to his feet. Whatever would be, would be. Denaro turned on his heel as if to leave.

"Denaro."

"Yes, sir?"

"Any news of Amber?"

A slight flush of color across the square-jawed face. "No, sir."

Why the color? Was Denaro embarrassed because he failed to have news of her—or because of other reasons? Colin put his hands in a pair of thigh pockets in his jumpsuit. "I need to have her located."

"Because of her background, she can be very ... elusive."

"I know. But she's under my protection, something I can't extend if I can't locate her." He was worried now, and it colored his tone.

Denaro drew himself up at the challenge. "I'll find her, sir."

"Good. Send Jonathan in as you leave, please." There was a cool draft through the apartment as Denaro left. Colin walked back to the exterior monitors and watched them—as close to an outer window as he could afford in his room. He thought of Amber and Jack and wondered where they were—and how they would all fare in the months ahead. Beside Denaro's news, he'd had word of yet another attack by the Ash-farel. They took no prisoners.

Chapter 17

It took Amber four weeks to break Winton's access code. She might never have thought of it, but if the name of the emperor he had helped depose opened the door lock, then the name of the man he owed most to and hated most would open his secret files: Pepys. There was a certain perverse logic to it. She knew that neither Pepys himself nor Vandover Baadluster would ever think of the code. It almost cost her her life to do it herself.

Winton's files were sketchy, almost in a short-hand, and she would have to be steeped in his mental processes to know most of what he had entered. They were not complete entries, but memory joggers. She did find a notation of Green Shirt activity and a search for a woman coded Countess. Winton's hunt had gone to ground just shortly before he'd left for Bythia, where he met his death.

She pored over the readouts, gleaning it for whatever he had recorded. His entries were short and cryptic. She came away knowing only that Countess had an aristocratic background and would be damned hard to find if she didn't want to be. The records confirmed that it was indeed the Green Shirts, with Winton as the prime manipulator, who'd shanghaied Jack as contract labor to the dead moon colony of Lasertown a few years ago. As a failed experiment, he was judged more dangerous to them alive than dead, and his shanghaiing had originally been a death sentence.

Even more rewarding was the revelation that Bythia had been intended as a death trap for Colin, either in direct conflict with Pepys over gaining access by the Walkers or by placing Colin into the role of a messianic figure in the Bythian culture. Instead, it had been Jack who'd fulfilled the prophecy and Winton who'd died.

It had not been Winton alone who'd thought of these machinations—but the partner was not identified.

She had just downed Winton's equipment when the automatic sentry came through the burned out Lunaii wing. The lights went out and she sat in the dark, pondering what she'd just read until:

"Halt! Remain in place and present your wrist ident."

Amber stifled her startled response. She wasn't going to give them a recording to make a voice-print from. With a movement that the sentry's infrared sensors would interpret as compliance, she swept a can from her belt and released its contents.

The spray had a dual purpose: its particles obscured the sentry's sensor readings and chilled her down instantly, making body heat temporarily unreadable as well. As far as the sentry was concerned, it had been blinded. She was getting old—she didn't jump it before its interference and assistance alarm went off.

She lashed out as she passed the machine in the corridor, her nails catching and half-ripping out the control board. It dangled from the sentry's body, but it was still functional enough to whip around and fire a stunning shot her direction.

It washed off the walls, an eerie blue light in the char. Amber gathered her heels under her and kept running, her pulse pounding in her throat, adrenaline roaring through her the way it used to when she ran the streets. Another sonic beam splashed the wall next to her. She winced as the backwash caught her arm, cramped in spasmodic response, shook it off, and barreled around a ruined corner.

She heard footsteps and knew the sentry's alarm had brought the palace police—WPs, Baadluster's men. Amber sucked in her breath and made a leap from the half-wall down the stairwell. She landed with a jar that froze her knees in pain, grinding her teeth together against the sudden agony she felt clear through her skull. The impact stopped her for a moment, then she gasped and bolted downstairs, her flight anything but noiseless.

She grabbed a band from about her black-sleeved wrist as she ran. The micro-recorder caught the sound of her feet upon the metal stairs. She rewound it and dropped it in the stairwell, broadcasting the sound on an endless loop, as she moved stealthily onto the ground floor corridor where fire had not gutted the wing.

Night lighting made the obsidite flooring glow

gently rose. She moved through it as though she walked barefoot over embers, eyeing doors as she passed them. She was trapped until she reached the corridor's end, where there would be access doors. Once there—Amber pushed discouraging thoughts out of her mind. Even if she could get through those doors, there would be no way she could keep her passage from being recorded.

Amber flattened herself to the wall and leaned out to eye the juncture. The door was open! It was closing slowly, grit or other minute obstacles in its track, retarding its slide. She threw secrecy to the wind and gained the door frame as it shut, catching a pinch of her shoe sole as she leaned outside.

Amber winced as she walked forward. The door had evidently caught her foot as well, it felt stone bruised at the heel. She wondered if the security cameras had caught enough of her to ID her. Jack would skin her alive for taking chances like this—if Pepys didn't catch her and skin her first. She rubbed her wrist, mourning the loss of some expensive equipment. Untraceable, of course, but regrettable nonetheless.

She took a deep breath and left the security of the building's shadow. Even as she pushed away, the floodlights blazed on, white-hot circles of betrayal in the night. Amber dodged blindly.

A huge hand wrapped about her elbow, drawing her into his umbra against the security floods.

"A second time ill-met, my lady Amber."

Her heart tumbled in her chest as K'rok drew her closer against his form. She could feel the rumble in his hairy chest as he said quietly,

"Your kind are not seeing well in the dark, I am thinking. Stand upon my feet and walk with me—they are seeing only my back."

He embraced her even more closely, walking her across the palace grounds. She heard shouts from behind, smelled his ursine, musky, and slightly rank odor. The beat of his heart (hearts?) sounded in her ear as he called back, "I've seen nothing—off-duty I am, and leaving."

A voice instructed him to take prisoner any unauthorized personnel he might encounter, adding, "If you please, Commander K'rok."

"I will!" Then, softly, "And it be pleasing me not."

"What are you doing?"

"Getting you away from here. You do not take warnings well."

"No."

K'rok made a noise that sounded like a growl. His immense, shaggy body dwarfed hers. He could snap her spine like a twig. "You should be knowing this by now. You must stay away."

"My business here is finished."

They were nearing the boundary sector, which was always well lit and patrolled. Amber faded into the overhanging branches of a tree, saying, "I'll be all right from here."

The lumbering Milot came to a halt. "I be thinking not. The Minister of War is no fool. Stay there. I will bring back a car." He loped away, shaggy head bent in determination.

Amber hugged the tree, bark scratching her chin. She found herself quaking in the aftermath of adrenal shock. She would have to trust K'rok, she had no one else to turn to within reach.

The car came to a halt. The door opened but a crack. She crawled along the ground and got in, twining her slim frame about K'rok's immense booted feet. In the shadowy interior, she was barely perceptible.

"Where to?"

"Under-Malthen. Any bar you want. I can alter the travel records." Her voice was muffled as she hid the paleness of her face in the crook of her black-sleeved arm.

K'rok grunted and jammed the car into motion. They were through the security gates and on the main thoroughfare when she heard the alarms go off, and all exits were closed.

The Milot let out an audible sigh, then rumbled down at his feet, "Are you going to stay there?"

"Yes," Amber said weakly. She doubted if she had the strength to move, just yet.

"Where will you go?"

"I don't know. Somewhere safe." She thought of Colin, and discarded it. Denaro was suspect, and Pepys knew she had sheltered with Colin before. She would not visit the emperor's scrutiny upon the Walker again, not for her sake. She lay hugging the Milot's boots and listening to the hovers whine in the floor under her ear, plotting her course. Suddenly, she knew where to have K'rok take her.

She had fallen asleep. K'rok nudged her gently a second time and Amber roused.

He growled, "After driving half the night, we appear to have arrived somewhere."

She sat up. The night was as dark as it could get, and the building before them stood immense, squat, and impregnable, white stone side catching what little glimmer was available from the moon. She saw the numerous security cameras, operating on filters, and smiled to herself. The woman she sought was still in residence here.

"What is it?" K'rok asked. "A tomb or temple?"

"No." She opened the car door. "Sadie is a pawnbroker." She pointed out the tunnel entrance. "This place is like an iceberg—four-fifths of it is underground." Amber shut the door and paused. "Thank you, commander," she said finally.

He nodded his head. "You are welcome. Tell me, if you would . . ." he stopped.

She knew what he wanted to ask. She smiled gently and said, "Last I heard he was still alive and kicking."

The Milot grinned hugely. "Thank you! And now, lady Amber, it is getting late. I must have time to get drunk enough to make my time away from the barracks to be believed.

She stepped away from the car and watched it whistle away, the immense frame of the Milot taking up the view through the back shield. Servos whined as cameras turned and stayed trained as she entered the tunnel gates.

"I have no appointment," Amber repeated for the tenth time. "I would just like to talk with Sadie and see if we can solve a problem I have." She stood wearily before the massive door, its overhead frame sculpted with the three ball symbol of the pawnbroker, and listened as the computer replied, "Madame is not to be disturbed—"

"Oh, but I am." The viewscreen filled with a massive woman, shot from the bosoms up, with dimples not only in her ample chins, but her bared shoulders as well. Sleep had tousled her dyed curls, but her eyes were far from puffy. Sadie eyed her alertly. "Who is it? Come out of the shadow there. I won't let you in if I can't identify you."

Amber put her shoulders back and stepped out, brushing her hood from her head, releasing her hair from its confinement as the woman muttered something about guests without manners and invitation disks.

Sadie stopped in mid-gesture. "Good heavens. Amber, is that you?"

"Yes, madam."

"Good heavens. The girl has become a woman. Where's Jack?"

She had already made certain plans while waiting for an audience. "Jack is dead."

"Posh. I know what the newscasts reported. Show me the body, and I'll believe Jack Storm is dead. I never saw a better survivor." The strangely alluring bulk of the woman adjusted on the couch. "What do you need, honey?"

"Sanctuary," Amber said, and fainted dead away on the doorstep.

Chapter 18

"I won't say your help's not appreciated," the base commander said, as they sat wearily down to eat in what was left of the mess. Soot darkened their faces. The work force hunched with bowed shoulders over cold rations, and their talk was muted with weariness. But they could afford to talk of victory, for the Thraks had been driven back, and only one Talon had been lost, along with a half-completed dome and two supply sheds. In the background, noise rumbled from bulldozers already back at work restoring the runways.

Staub added, "But you present me with a problem. Policy tells me that I cannot let you go free."

"I want to stay," Jack said. He paused with his fork in hand as Skal added, "Let me near a river and you cannot keep me." The otterlike tail twitched in emphasis.

The commander looked at Skal. "You, sir, as a representative of local government, should be treated as an ambassador. However, since we're not here in any official capacity. . . ." the auburn-haired man let his voice trail off and shrugged.

"You would have no capacity if we had not intervened," the Fisher returned. He looked down at his plate and stirred the rations into a stew, meat, fruit, and vegetable compounds unrecognizable. Then he lifted a forkful, sniffed delicately, and began to eat. "Might you have beer?"

Staub's hazel eyes looked a bit glazed but he said hastily. "Yes, of course. The refrigeration section was undamaged by the strafing." He snapped his fingers and a string bean of an adjutant took his request.

"With all due respect," Jack interrupted, drawing the commander's attention back to him, "I don't see how you can afford to refuse any help you can get. Consider my performance against the Thraks a demonstration of armor's capabilities. I know you can appreciate that."

"I can appreciate it, but I can't trust it." Staub was a man of easy authority, broad-shouldered, with a thick waist that might later tend toward roundness but now was flat. Despite the red hair, he had a complexion that tanned nicely, and the sun had etched a network of wrinkles about his gray-green eyes. He was apparently ten years Jack's senior. He had workman's hands: square, competent, solid. He drummed the tabletop for emphasis now with his left. "We've been told to look out for you, Storm. Word is you're operating as Pepys' agent."

As Skal spewed a mouthful of food back onto his plate, Jack said smoothly, "I'm dead, as far as Pepys knows."

"I remember you," the commander said. "The business at Lasertown was reported as underground. You have a reputation for doing an agent's work."

Jack smiled at the irony. Everything he'd done at Lasertown had been in his own interest. Pepys had downplayed the entire situation, neither disavowing it nor claiming it in his own interest. But telling the tale was not something he had time for. Staub was unsure, it was time to convince him before he made his mind up.

The aide returned with three cartons of beer. Skal made a great deal of noise opening his up before lifting the now foaming container to his muzzle. Jack took advantage of the break in conversation.

"I'd have come to you the conventional way, with even more suits, but I was ambushed at Gibbon's on Malthen."

There was a sparkle deep in Staub's eyes, but he, too, turned his attention to the beer, saying, "Who?"

Jack ignored him. "Then I found my way to Skagboots' Retreads on Victor Three. Bootsie was very interested in my armor, but we got interrupted by a routine freebooters' strafing run."

Staub looked amused. "It sounds hazardous to be conversing with you."

Jack looked up at the great rent overhead in the mess hall. "I think you're done for the day," he answered.

"Mm." The commander paused for a moment, took some updated damage reports from his aide, made some decisions and delegations, then turned his attention back to Jack. "It's a long way from Skagboots' to here."

Skal bared his too sharp teeth. "That was my fault, commander. I intercepted him and asked him to come with me. My world had a . . . pest problem . . . I was most anxious to solve."

"Meaning us?"

The Fisher nodded.

"I see." Staub took a deep drink of his beer. He made a face as he swallowed. "We've been dumping excess fuel and duds before coming back in to land. It's a sloppy habit. I apologize, Skal, to you and your Elders. I'll send out cleanup details, if you'll allow us to set up an official dump."

"What does he mean?"

"He means a plane can't come in safely carrying overallowances of fuel or firepower. It's usually jettisoned over uninhabited areas . . . swamp or marshland. But," and here Jack scratched his temple where his eyebrow met it, "all of Mistwald is swamp or marshy. They're used to having filtration islands set up in those bog areas, to pick up the toxics. . . ."

"The method you talked to me about."

"Yes."

Skal laid his tail on the table, the portion that would reach. The gesture unnerved both Jack and the Green Shirt commander. The Fisher stroked his pelt, which was as sleek there as anywhere. He looked up. "The location is different and may be difficult to reach, but it is all one body," he said. "My grooming is as important here as anywhere." He curled the tip. "There *is* no backwater on Mistwald."

"I see what you mean." Staub reached for his beer quickly as Skal lashed his tail back, nearly upsetting the cartons. "Your—ah—point is well taken. Chrysler!"

The string bean of an aide leaned down.

"Get cleanup details formed as soon as possible. We've been polluting major waterways."

The aide nodded and left the mess.

Skal finished his rations and looked about appraisingly. He noticed the empty place setting at Staub's elbow and pointed his fork at it. "My condolences, commander, for the death of an honored one."

The redhead looked quickly, then shook his head. "That's not because of the raid. It's for the founders of the movement. We lost our leadership to the Sand Wars."

"Yet you carry on."

"In our way, though—" Staub halted abruptly, noticed the listening silence around the long table and smiled. "The Green Shirts do whatever they can."

"You didn't get where you are today by not taking chances. Can you afford to turn me and what I offer down?"

"If you're a beacon by which Pepys locates this base, I can't afford to keep you." The man met Jack's eyes with a level stare of his own. "What is worth the risk?"

"I can give you Pepys' head on a platter."

There was a startled silence throughout the mess, then Staub put his head back and laughed, breaking the tension, and Jack could hear the babble of excited voices start again.

When Staub quieted, he said, "Make a martyr

of the emperor and we will never replace the chain of command."

"Of course not. But I can give you evidence first that will erode public confidence in him—start an outcry that will demand he be replaced."

"You're a Knight. Why would you want to do such a thing?"

"Because," Jack said, leaning forward on an elbow, "I didn't swear to Pepys. I was sworn to Regis."

Disbelief flickered across the commander's face. "Regis? Impossible. That was—what—twenty-five years ago? You're scarcely older than that. You'd have to be my age."

"How long have you been a Green Shirt?"

Skal sat back in his chair, holding his beer close to his chest, enjoying the conversation.

"Since the Sand Wars," Staub answered Jack.

"I don't know how the chain of command works here," Storm continued. "Or how long you've been underground. There was a captain of the Knights who spoke to the Dominion Congress last year, before the Alliance."

Staub's attention sharpened. "There were rumors."

"Good ones. I was that captain, soon to be a commander."

"The one found in cold sleep?"

"Yes, I was found on that transport, the only one who lived to tell the tale."

"My God." Staub pushed away from the table as if denying it and all that he had heard. "It's impossible."

"You heard the rumors." Jack wet his throat with the last of his beer, and waited.

"Then where have you been?"

"Staying alive," Jack answered. "At first, the Green Shirts who found me hid me for reasons of their own . . . and then I found it safer to hide under the hem of the emperor's own robe. Learning who betrayed us on Milos . . . who betrayed us throughout the Sand Wars. I was betrayed again when we allied with the Thraks."

"We were all betrayed," a smoke-hoarse voice threw in.

Jack nodded. "And now that I've learned what I have, it's time to take action, but I need help for that."

Staub stood up. "If you're telling the truth, you've one hell of a story."

"And if he isn't, commander, we can take care of him later." A wing captain, two seats back from Jack, spoke up. He drew his commander's attention.

"And if I am," Jack said, "I can give you what the Green Shirts desperately need: public sympathy, Dominion support."

"How?"

Jack paused. "We raid Klaktut."

The commander's laugh was short and bitter. "Now I know you *are* crazy. You Knights lost your asses in there last year. Raiding a crèche planet? You're lucky the Thraks didn't slaughter every one of you."

"What you don't know is that Pepys told them we were coming."

"What?"

Jack nodded. "They were waiting for us. We did a lot of damage anyway—gave them a show of strength that Pepys was counting on. It was that raid which made Tricatada decide to propose the Alliance. But what Pepys didn't count on was what we saw."

Staub sat down again, slowly. He wet his lips in apprehension. "What . . . did you see?"

"Farms of humans, bred for food and slaughter. People we assumed lost to the Sand Wars, still alive. Hopeless, but alive. We knew the Thraks were murderers. We didn't know they were human eaters." Jack stood up, raising his voice. "There is a story of courage and misery in every captive we bring back—a story of a life that was betrayed so that Pepys might bring down Regis and gain a throne. And even for those we can't bring back, a clean death might be a mercy."

"I can't . . . I can't authorize a deepspace action," Staub said. He scrubbed a rough hand through his auburn hair.

"But you want to."

"Yes. Yes, by damn. I'll take you to Klaktut."

"Then get authorization."

Staub looked to Skal. "That means more cradles and a larger base."

The Fisher shrugged. "If you can keep it clean, as Jack has told me you can, I see no reason why the Elders would not agree. As long as it is temporary."

Staub gave a savage grin. "Then excuse me, gentlemen. I have a call to put through."

Chapter 19

The pawnbroker's home was gracious inside, crowded with remnants of other days, some beautiful and some homely, all of them precious in their antiquity. Amber glided through the clutter with pantherlike grace. It was a game she had played before—how close could her cuff or sleeve come to toppling something without actually touching it? Sadie's eyes glittered as she watched her guest. Amber kept her half-smile hidden behind a curtain of tawny hair and came to a stop, kneeling at her hostess' chaise.

The woman touched her head in what might have been a caress. "Feeling better, I see?"

"Definitely."

"I'm sorry not to have had time to see you these past few days. I've been busy."

"And I'm sorry to have been an uninvited guest."

"But not unwelcome," Sadie said. Her voice was rich and full, almost fruity. "You've got trouble. Vandover Baadluster and St. Colin of the Blue Wheel are both looking for you. Baadluster worries me, but Colin does not. Which one of them are you hiding from?"

Amber rocked back from her knees and settled cross-legged on her rump, a more comfortable position. She shrugged. "Baadluster."

"Ah." Her eyes were a dark brown, almost black, and seemed to focus on some distant sight, as she sat for a time, deep in thought. Then she said slowly, "Even Pepys does not bother me unnecessarily. You'll be safe here. The question is: how long?"

"That's a good question," Amber answered. "I don't know."

"You'll be wanting to make other arrangements?"

She wondered what the other woman was thinking as Sadie gestured with her hands, her nails done in gold and diamond overlay. Her crimson lips were permanently tinted and her eyes indelibly outlined. Her bulk reigned over the chaise with a majesty all its own. Yet this woman was, indisputably, powerful and dangerous. "I don't have any place else to go," Amber admitted in a small voice. "I've been out of under-Malthen too long. You're the only one I can trust."

"I see." Sadie gave a full and generous smile. "Everything has its price."

"I can't tap my accounts. Vandover would trace me immediately."

"Money is not an immediate problem. Jack even has a small account he's left open with me, just in case. But I have needs, too, Amber. You are a young lady of many talents."

She sensed the change in tone. Her back straightened. "You need my help."

Sadie caressed the back of one hand with the

palm of the other. "Yes. For which I would pay you, against the cost of your sanctuary."

Amber knew that Sadie knew her reputation for thievery. Once here, hidden behind (underneath) these solid walls, she didn't want to stray, but she did not dare refuse a request if Sadie made one. She inclined her head. "I'll do whatever I can. When will you have . . . arrangements . . . made?"

"Arrangements?" Sadie's eyes widened slightly. Then she laughed, a full-throated laugh of the variety men liked. "Dear, I'm not asking you to steal for me."

"You're not?"

"No! I need you to work in the morgue."

Jack lay in his hammock and listened to the barely audible hum of the cruiser. He'd been given a private cubicle, but if he wished to do anything more vigorous than sneeze, he'd have to leave the area. The overhead lights were dimmed to downtime, and he'd been asleep. But now he was awake, sweat-soaked and uneasy with his dreams of Thraks and *sand* wars and death still vivid in his mind. The cruiser held a wing of Talons in its gut. This was no heavily supported invasion. They were going in to make a quick strike—hit and run—they had almost as much video equipment as they did weapons. Commander Staub had agreed with Jack that the raid's main purpose would be to decommission one of the major nests and obtain the footage necessary to discredit Pepys.

He ought to be sleeping well, with thoughts of

revenge for company. Jack absently patted his vest down, searching one of its many pockets for *mordil*. The vial was empty except for a glistening coat of liquid. He unstoppered it and tilted the last few drops onto his tongue. He closed his eyes and drifted, wondering if the drug would put him back to sleep.

In his half-awake thoughts, he sought comfort and found Bogie, The alien/suit was in equipment storage, resting comfortably. The helmet's solars had enough energy to keep him growing and Jack had ample opportunity to keep them charged.

Despite the voice synthesizer, Bogie had not become particularly articulate. But Jack found himself reaching a kindred spirit when they communed in this manner.

The sentience had also been thinking of war, though his memories were vaguer. He was eager and certain of victory and communicated that to Jack. *Come fight with me.*

"Fight who?"

Does it matter? The world is full of enemies and victory.

Jack walked the landscape of another world, the suit striding by his side, its normal opalescence replaced by a golden aura. That aura was Bogie's berserker spirit and it blazed so keenly Jack felt its warmth on his flank, as though he marched with a being made of fire.

"I don't like killing."

What about honor?

Jack halted. He looked around him. The landscape was so otherworldly, he knew that if he walked here in actuality, he would need environmental gear. "Bogie—I can't judge well enough to know who is being honorable and who isn't. We have a saying—there's two sides to every moon."

Meaning?

"The dark side of a moon is not dark because it's evil. It's dark because it faces away from the sun and we don't see it illuminated. Rotate the axis and the positions are exchanged. Is one more honorable than the other?"

The suit's aura ebbed and flared. *It is difficult to know.*

"Exactly."

Then where is the honor in war?

"I suppose it comes from fighting for something you believe in."

Bogie was silent for a while. Then he stopped and extended a glove toward Jack. *You are older.*

"I . . . think so."

You decide who to fight.

"Right now, it's Thraks."

He felt a rush of fury, and the aura extended around them both. *The enemy!*

It was that fury that made it possible for Jack to wear the armor. He embraced it, let it blaze in him as well. Before the fire died back, he was asleep in dreamless depths.

The klaxons woke him. He disentangled himself from the hammock, head throbbing from the *mordil*. Running footsteps filled the corridor. He slid his door back as he shrugged into boots. They slept clothed.

"What is it?"

"Unidentifieds closing in. We're on general quarters alert."

Jack grabbed his pack and followed. Bulkheads closed down behind him, securing the cruiser's sector they occupied. The hold was crowded with men, waiting, watching the monitor. Staub's face filled it.

"We are being pursued by a three-wing force of unidentifieds. Our speed is not yet sufficient to attain FTL, therefore, we remain on full battle alert. Expect an exchange of fire as they do not answer the hailing frequency."

Damn. Jack watched as the screen went to neutral. So much for sneaking up on the Thrakian League's backyard.

He half-turned and was surprised to find Chrysler, the adjutant, at his side. The lanky man grimaced.

"Bad luck."

"I'll say. Worse luck if the on-board computers can't make 'em."

Jack felt his eyebrows arch. "What have we got running us?"

"The best we could steal. We may not have much, but what we've got is the best." The adjutant's eyes were bloodshot from having been awakened and he blinked rapidly. "Number Two is too far away to do us any good."

There had been a second cruiser launched, but not from Mistwald. It had coordinates to meet them "turning the corner" just before they went into Klaktut. Jack had no doubt that Number

Two was being told of the problem, Staub was that kind of commander.

The screen activated abruptly. Staub had deep lines about his jaw. "The unidentifieds have been made, gentlemen. We're looking at Ash-farel."

The hold became hushed.

The commander went on, "We have no information regarding in-flight attacks. We're still trying to open a com line between us."

"We'll outrun them," an unseen man at Jack's back said.

Jack knew better. As if in response, Staub continued, "They're closing fast. Rig for evasive tactics and return fire. If we can't talk to them, we're going to shoot first."

Jack began shoving his way through the press of men, to reach the two-way com on the monitor. Before he could gain it, there was a massive explosion and the hold rocked violently. Jack kept his feet. The Ash-farel could swat at them as if they were gnats. He knew. But he had never expected it to happen. He'd seen the aliens strike at Thraks, but never at anyone else.

He slapped the monitor and opened the line. "Don't fire back! It's our only hope!"

"Who is this?"

"Jack Storm."

Staub winced as the cruiser shook violently with a second blast. The klaxons began. "They didn't give us a chance, Storm," he answered. "Damage control report." Behind him, Jack could see the blurred outlines of the bridge. "Gentlemen, it appears we'll fight the Thraks some other time. Abandon ship."

Chrysler had come through the crowd at Jack's elbow. "Come on, sir, there's no time to waste. We don't know how many escape pods are operational."

Jack was at the bulkhead as it unsealed the hold. He started down the left corridor, but Chrysler caught at him. The wiry fingers were like bands of steel about his arm. "This way."

"My armor."

"We've no room for equipment!"

He shook Chrysler off. The cruiser shuddered a third time, like a dying animal, and blue-gray smoke abruptly filled the corridor. Jack would never make it to the equipment lockers in that direction.

He staggered after Chrysler, even as Bogie awoke in his thoughts.

Boss! I'm in trouble! The hold's on fire.

Jack had no time to answer him, as men pulled and tugged, jostled and carried him almost bodily down the corridor to the escape boats.

Boss . . .

Jack tried to dig in his heels. The river of men swarmed through a bulkhead, its framework jammed halfway open. He stumbled and went down. His last thought was that he was going to be trampled, but then he felt Chrysler's hard hands upon him, and he was being dragged through and thrown into a small compartment.

Jack sat up and spat out a mouthful of blood. He ground his teeth experimentally as the pod began to vibrate, preparatory to ejection. It was a two-man unit and he knew without looking that Chrysler was his companion.

Without shame, he hung his head and wept as the pod jettisoned, and the wounded cruiser fell away behind them, blazing in the velvet of deep space, Bogie trapped within its wreckage.

Chapter 20

The cryogenic vaults below Sadie's were not a morgue, but they felt like it. Cold, still, with bodies laid out on slabs, some with the modesty of a shroud, but many not, covered only by their lid. Amber walked among them with her keypad, noting vital statistics as their medical monitors gave continuous readouts.

Despite the warmth of her clothing and the delicate gloves pulled over her tapered fingers, she was chilled. She did not like the deathly quiet and never would. But the alternative Sadie had offered her was better than being one of the chilled down bodies lying here. She'd done it twice and hoped never to do it again, not unless it was to follow Jack across the stars.

Some of the inhabitants here were collateral, held against loans owed Sadie. She would not keep anyone in cold sleep more than two years so the loans were more often than not made in desperation, and the relative asleep was probably getting the kinder end of the bargain. Malthen was not gentle to the destitute.

There were cryo vaults in the rich end of town, where one could put down ten years or so, to

keep off the wrinkles. More time was not advised—
like Jack's, locked in the same mind-loop of
dreams for seventeen years—the mind was affected. Amber knew of more than one high roller
who'd accepted cold sleep as an alternative to
bankruptcy—out of control finances careened to
a halt and the interest earned over five or six
years could bring a family back from debt.

And then, of course, there was always the sad
tale of a sleeper who awoke to find his credit
embezzled.

Amber prayed the readings stayed constant.
She disliked the hard-faced nurse/tech and the
woman stayed away unless the readouts became
erratic. This was the last place Amber wanted to
be found. Of course, the cryo machinery fed into
its mainframe system, but Sadie kept her own
records. Amber likened it to having a second set
of books. She was fairly certain that all the
information gathered and recorded would be
brought to use someday. Sadie took painstaking
effort to gather new data and match it to the
correct sleeper. She had a fortune resting in these
vaults and knew it.

It was the only set of records on Malthen that
Amber hadn't tapped into yet—had not even
thought of tapping into, until Sadie mentioned
the morgue. Sadie was more than a money changer
and less than a pawnbroker—she could occasionally act as a fence. The only Countess Amber
knew lifted jewels once in a while. She was certain Sadie had to have done business with her.
And, perhaps, Sadie had also crossed paths with

an aristocratic woman who was a major power in the Green Shirts.

Her time was limited. Sadie would find out soon that her job was done, and the merchandise she'd been told to steal was waiting at a neutral delivery station. It was now or never if she wanted to get into Sadie's records. Amber left the lab floor and went to the computer room which was pleasingly warm. She let the keypad transcribe to the mother computer while she thawed out. As the data flow filled the system, she sat back and relaxed.

Sadie's work was routine, even boring stuff. Basically it was manually facilitated data entry. Hidden inside it was another program, much more insidious, intended to break the memory bank lockdown on files. Amber chewed on a thumbnail and watched the screen. She checked her time and kept on chewing.

The curtain brought down across Bogie's contact with Jack was black and sudden. The cruiser had ceased to convulse under enemy fire and was adrift, and the alien could sense fires raging inside its hulk. The cargo hold stayed dark and cold—the sprinkler system had damped out an earlier flare and now was all quiet.

Bogie could not remember a time when he'd been alone, severed from Jack's mind. There had been several times when the contact had been incomprehensible, but never totally unavailable. He was afraid. Could their fight be finished when it had hardly begun?

A metallic clank sounded throughout the framework of the cruiser. Bogie brought the suit to attention at the noise. It was a vibration that trilled for long moments, followed by a series of clanks. Something nudged at the cruiser. Then he heard the sound of air locks recycling and knew the vessel was being boarded.

Jack had come back. Bogie's thoughts heated with welcome, then cooled. The presence he encountered entering the cruiser had no similarity to Jack's. Bogie recoiled from the thought. Nothing found alive on the cruiser would be left that way. All equipment was to be examined and salvaged.

To the beings approaching him now, Bogie was life destined to be exterminated.

But first, they might strip from him the means of his existence before letting him die . . . slowly, under inspection.

Bogie shuddered. To have come so far from death into life, to be reduced to . . . this. Within the shell of the armor of a Dominion Knight, the alien shrank in fear. Silently, he cried for aid and received no answer.

The screen came alive. Amber leaned forward and began to run her inquiries. She looked at the information coming up silently. She downed the file and brought up another one. This was not data the sleeper would willingly give anyone.

Amber swiveled in her chair. She looked through the office window at the sleepers in their bays. There was only one possibility that could obtain the information she was bringing up.

Sadie was running debriefing loops on the cold

sleepers. Illegal as hell—and probably worth every credit of the risk. Anything the sleeper had ever done or thought up until that moment of chilldown was encoded on tape. It might be difficult to decode in its entirety, by anyone but the sleeper, but Sadie had dredged a few incidents out on the files Amber read. It was rape of the most insidious kind . . . yet. . . .

What were the odds that the Countess had ever been here? And even as she thought that, the cold realization went through her that Sadie had tapes on her—as she was before Hussiah on Bythia had purged her of her ability to murder with her mind.

She could gain it back—all of it, all of the subliminal programming with unknowable targets for her assassin talents—just by submitting herself to the tape again. The same type of information Jack was looking for on himself, held by the Green Shirts, the mind-loop to a past thought lost.

That shock held her in trance a split second too long to react to the presence in the doorway.

A rich, contralto voice said, "You do a job well and quickly, but I'm not impressed if this is how you repay me."

Chapter 21

Amber turned to meet the harsh and prey-
ing glare of Sadie. Amber stood up, gathering
herself.

"You're a rapist," she said. "I've met street
trash before, but this—"

"This is insurance," Sadie interrupted. "And I
don't believe that you're in any position to judge
me, my girl. Is this why you came to me? Why
you pleaded for me to take you in? Or is this an
afterthought?"

"This," Amber said wryly, "is why I needed
to come here. Only I was tapping Pepys' files."

The woman's full mouth opened in astonish-
ment. Then, abruptly, Sadie dimpled. "My," she
said. "You're still full of surprises. Shut that
down and come upstairs, then. It's too cool down
here for me."

"I need to find someone."

"I have a terminal upstairs. If I feel it's justi-
fied and worth the price—and you can pay the
price—we'll talk." With amazing grace for her
size, Sadie turned in the doorway.

Amber felt it wise to obey her and followed.

*　　*　　*

Number Two found them after only three days adrift. By then, Jack had seen the Ash-farel bring in a tow, put tractor beams on the wreckage, and haul it away. He'd already lost Bogie when that happened, but he screened his portal dark and refused to watch as the mysterious enemy left them as quickly as they had come. The sundering he felt was as complete as death and what he felt went beyond mourning, for with the alien's passing, he lost the last link to what had been his life before his betrayal in the Sand Wars.

And a Knight never lost his armor. Never. Not unless he were dead first. He was party to one of the ultimate disgraces. He had lost his armor, and he had purposely disarmed the deadman switch, leaving the suit vulnerable to whatever enemy wished to examine it. The Ash-farel did not know it yet, but they had a prize beyond reckoning. And what would they make of the tattered piece of dead flesh within it?

The pods were not fired upon as the enemy left. Chrysler sat hunched into the tiny bodyrest in front of the few manual controls the vessel had and watched in horrified fascination. Over and over he kept repeating: "Why don't they come after us? We're just sitting here, going nowhere. Why don't they come finish us off?" until Jack snapped, "Shut up" at him. Then the aide sat in shock and did not rouse until the tracker showed another vessel incoming.

The pods were scooped up one by one—and the three bigger lifeboats. In all, only two men from the cruiser were unaccounted for in addition to those dead from the direct hit. Storm was given another cubicle, a ration for bathing, a hot meal, and told to report to the map room.

Staub was already there, eyes sunk deep in a face bruised with fatigue, talking to another Green Shirt with an unmistakably military bearing. They looked up as Jack came in.

"Jack, this is Captain Tronski. Tron, this is the man who gave us our target."

"Wish I had known the Ash-farel were in the same quadrant," Jack said.

They gripped hands. Tron released first, with a thin-lipped smile. He had the kind of face that ran to fat even though the rest of his body was square and compact. He wore khaki and his gray and beige hair was cropped short and neat. Thick, wiry eyebrows shaded eyes of light brown. He looked down at the star charts coming up on the tablescreen.

He tapped a sector. "We think they came out of here, but there's no way to be sure with FTL. We don't even know if they knew we were here, or if they saw an opportunity and took it."

Jack looked at Staub. "Did you get a shot off?"

The commander shook his head. "Not a one. They had the momentum—they closed with incredible speed."

"With that kind of speed, they were probably getting ready to jump off, themselves."

Tron's eyebrows did a sort of dance. "That's what I thought."

"Where would they be going from here?"

"Outward Bounds or, to the other angle, Klaktut."

Staub licked cracked lips. "That leaves us with

a problem, gentlemen. Do we want to proceed to our original destination if the Ash-farel are there as well?"

Jack added quietly, "Or do we want to proceed at all."

Staub and Tron said together, "We're going in to fight."

"But most of the video equipment is lost on Number One."

The two Green Shirts looked at him. He recognized a kind of weighing in their expressions. "I see. If we can't get evidence against Pepys, the least we can do is pose as treaty breakers. He'll still have trouble."

Staub nodded. "That's it precisely, Jack. We've got enough weaponry here to arm the men rescued from Number One as well. Our original objective is impossible, but we can still do Pepys a lot of damage."

"And get our boys out of there?" As Jack spoke, his mind raced furiously. He would be going into a Thrakian nest virtually naked without his armor. How could he even contemplate such a thing? These men had no idea what they were up against.

"I won't bandy numbers with you. We know our losses are going to be severe—but we've got enough Talons to pick up survivors."

Jack looked at Tron. "This is a suicide mission with those odds."

The two men looked at their star chart, and Staub said quietly, "It's all they've left us with. But it's better than nothing."

His pulse pounded in his ears, deafening him,

and in his memory, he seemed to recalled a bullet-faced drill instructor, glaring at him and a thousand other recruits, saying, "No suit, no soldier."

Time to prove the lie.

Jack said, "I've got a water credit begging to be used. If you'll excuse me for the moment, I'll see you in staging."

Colin stood in the isolation of his Walker apartment, mentally taking leave. As he gazed at his furnishings, he realized that he only owned two things he regretted leaving behind: his porcelain tea set and his redwood table. The porcelain would never survive the subtle vibrations of space and subspace drive, the redwood table was simply too heavy to take along.

A man his age, and that was all he had accumulated. Colin smiled sadly. It was all he'd needed, really. As a man of God, the other furnishings were only temporary conveniences.

He was leaving things left undone, and he hoped Jack Storm would forgive him for that. Amber had been located hiding with money changer Sadie: there were locks on those doors even Pepys did not dare try to open. The young woman would be safe there until Sadie wearied of her presence.

"Sir?" Denaro stood in the doorway, waiting for him.

Colin sighed. "Just saying good-bye."

"You'll be back."

"Of course." But Colin had never doubted that before. He picked up his briefcase. "I take it Jonathan is downstairs leaving last minute memos for Margaret?"

Denaro nodded. He wore an expression Colin could not read, as the prelate brushed past him and into the corridor. "Have you done what I told you?"

"Yes. Amber will get word that Jack has reached a Green Shirt installation on Mistwald, and she won't be able to trace it back to us. But I don't understand how you know—"

"It's not for you to understand everything I do." He pressed the young man's hand. "I am not a Green Shirt, Denaro, but even you must know the Walker conscience is far-reaching."

Surprise washed over Denaro's handsome face as Colin reached the lift. That was as close as the saint had come to explaining himself for some time. But, Colin thought as the vehicle moved downward, not even Denaro understood why he was making the journey he was. Star maps and charts had been spread all over Colin's quarters for days, and the young militant was as mystified as ever.

So, Colin hoped, would the others be, their minds and thoughts rooted in subspace and FTL. Only he could stand earthbound and see the pattern. And see the pattern he had. And wondered momentarily if he was right in keeping it to himself, but he did not wish the pattern disrupted. He alone knew where the Ash-farel would strike next, and he intended to be there.

As he reached the lobby, Jonathan was standing, worry pressed into his face as visibly as his wrinkles, his bulky form obscuring the lobby monitoring screens.

"The emperor is on the line, your holiness. He would like an audience with you."

"Tell him my corsair is waiting. We don't want to miss departure time."

Jonathan frowned heavily. Colin noted with surprise the fringe of gray winging its way into his temples. "His majesty has already told me to tell you that he can postpone that departure—indefinitely."

So his old friend was going to be difficult. Colin looked upstairs, regretting having left the privacy of his apartment behind. But he did not want to return to it, not even for this conversation. He was afraid that, if he returned to it, he would never wish to leave it. For the sake of the Walker colonies, he must not do that.

"Very well. Set up a screen. I'd like this to be as private as possible."

Denaro said, "I'll be outside with the transport."

Colin looked at him as he passed, reminding the militant, "There's to be no trouble with the guard."

The young man looked at him. He fingered the wooden cross about his neck. "No," he said quietly. "No trouble with the Thraks. This time."

Jonathan was huffing as he ordered up a screen. He stopped long enough to look after Denaro. "He's been getting insolent."

Colin stepped through the booth's sonic walls, but not before he said to Jonathan, "It's the hot blood. He'll be all right."

His right-hand man frowned but could say nothing more, for Colin had passed the boundary of hearing. The monitor came on as soon as Colin seated himself.

"Good morning, Pepys," he said to the man who'd been caught unawares, looking away, his red hair in a frenzy of static activity. "How may I be of service to you today?"

"Cut the bullshit, Colin. What are you up to?"

"I am up to my neck in colonies threatening to sue for the protection of the Triad Throne. And you?"

Pepys, his cat-green eyes glittering, made a noncommittal noise, then added, "I'm up to my neck in Thraks."

"That appears to have been a choice you made."

"It does, doesn't it. Why are you leaving our fair Malthen?"

"I'm taking a constitutional. We still have one, haven't we?"

Pepys stared directly into Colin's eyes. The corner of his mouth twitched, but whether for a shout or a smile, Colin couldn't guess.

Then the emperor said, "I'm but a fisherman of stars. One or two are bound to escape the net."

Jonathan signaled outside the transparent barrier that the time was up. Colin looked briefly to him, then back to the emperor.

"You have no reason to hold me, Pepys."

"What about treason?"

Colin answered mildly, "If you really thought so, you wouldn't be calling me. You'd have the troops here picking me up. I don't covet your empire and you know that."

Pepys leaned back in his crimson and gold

robes. He plucked idly at the hem of one cuff. "The Walkers existed before you and will exist after."

"I should hope so."

"Damn it, Colin, stop pushing me. If your colonies wish to be annexed, I don't see the harm to you. It's not as if they were recanting their faith as well."

Colin leaned forward to the screen. He wanted to be very sure Jonathan could not read his lips. "There is a kingdom beyond that of yours, Pepys, and that is the kingdom of God. A kingdom where taxes are not for warfare and ego, but for works toward the good of man. Push me further and I will go to the Dominion for aid."

"They'll never answer your call."

"Don't try to fool me into believing you underestimate me. We both know better."

Pepys fell silent. Then. "If I . . . back off, will you stay?"

"No. Not now. I can't just yet. I have some investigating to do."

The emperor sat bolt upright. "Good god, man, are you going after the Ash-farel?"

"You know the Walker tenets as well as I. If God's Son walked beyond, who knows where He stepped? Perhaps even the mysterious Ash-farel have heard of His passage."

"Colin, I—"

"We're losing our departure window," Colin said stonily. "Let me go."

"Colin—"

"Emperor!" And the religious leader of a vast estate raised his voice to a whipcrack.

Pepys slumped. He waved a hand. "Very well. This is not the time or place for us to wrestle. But one day, we will find out who wields the most power."

Colin did not answer. He bolted from the privacy booth, gathering up Jonathan, saying, "Hurry, before he changes his mind."

Chapter 22

The wreckage of the battle cruiser reverberated as the Ash-farel took it apart plate by plate. Bogie stayed in the equipment hold and shuddered as each metal-ringing clang brought them closer. His sensors told him of the radiation and decontaminant solution treatment each section was getting before they scrapped it. Nothing alive would remain when the aliens were done—not even him.

He kept the night screen visor down, giving his cameras some vision although the backup lights had gone long ago. He shuddered. Darkness was the same as death to him. He was hungry and alone. He thought of Amber. Would he survive to tell her of Jack's fate? There was a time when he could have reached out and brushed Amber's thoughts, but she had changed. Unless she was with him, her thoughts were not to be found. He was utterly bereft.

There was a scritch along the flooring. Bogie looked down, scanning. The viewscreens picked up a form. He searched his memory for it—a rodent, he thought. He flexed the armor and bent down to retrieve it. The creature gave a frightened screech and bolted away. It was quick, too quick for him. Jack had a blinding speed and grace in the armor that Bogie alone did not. Ruefully, he watched the creature sprint through the hold, dodging crates of equipment.

As though the sound of something alive in the hold had alerted them, the doors wrenched opened, and a blinding arc of light shone in. Bogie's sensors were dazzled. Blinded, he could not see the Ash-farel coming in. He could only hope—pray, the word came to memory that Jack used—that the armor shielded him from the aliens. He could only pray that he lived through the coming ordeal.

Jack remembered where the main crèche was. He'd brought them down almost on top it, and watched the Thraks swarm out of the mud-caked opening as he guided the parasail down. The sky was full of troopers. There were spits of orange as those carrying flamethrowers started them up even before they touched down. Jack knew one of the troopers. He had publicly stated his intention to glide over the nest, firing, before he hit ground.

It was a suicidal maneuver, but if it worked, it would give them all precious time.

He began to swing as the parallel settled down. He had both hands full collapsing the chute and shucking the harness, but he loaded up with grenades when he came up running. He'd told them what to expect, but they froze anyway at the sight of the fenced, green grass farms, and the mindless humans running naked alongside the rails to watch the action.

"Move it, move it, move it! Film it if you've got equipment, but move it!" The cords on his throat stood out as he shouted.

A trooper looked at him, and blinked.

It was the last move he made. A wave of Thraks topped the grassy knoll and one of the lopers to the fore took the Green Shirt's head off. Jack threw a grenade and rolled for cover. Dirt clods and grass divots and hard bits of shell rained through the air. He got up cautiously, unslung his rifle from his back, and went looking for trouble.

The mud-daub nest of the Thraks loomed aboveground, a landlocked iceberg of dried clay. Below, it might spread out concentrically for half a mile. He was probably running over tunnels now— before, with the weight and power of the armor, he'd dropped in. Now, the only way he could get in was if they dragged him in. . . .

It was a bad idea. He checked his watch. The chronos told him he had fifteen minutes left on the assault. Then the Talons were landing or hooking up everyone fit to retreat. He was either with them, or he wasn't.

A Thraks reared up in front of him, chitin and carapaces rattling with anger. The Kabuki mask of a face clacked and chittered at him, russet and brown, faceted red eyes aglow with battle lust. It was too close to fire, the backwash would clip it as well, so it lunged and caught Jack by the wrists. Instead of resisting, Jack gave, crumpling, and the Thraks overbalanced. Jack kicked it in the stomach region and sent it the rest of the way over. It opened its mandibles in protest and Jack dropped a grenade down its thorax.

It choked on the bomb. Jack got up and ran as the beast thrashed and gagged. It was almost a mercy when the grenade went off.

He checked his crossed ammo belts. He had five grenades left. The orange wash of flame-throwers caught his gaze as he vaulted a fence. The nest was cracked open like a ripe melon. Men and Thraks were dying by the dozens.

Jack stopped and swallowed. A twig cracked near his flank, he whirled, and the dumb stare of a trio of cattle met his. He flapped his arms at them. "Get out of here! Go on!"

The woman stared a second longer after the two males bolted. Her breasts were dirty dugs that hung down to her waist, for all her youth. Up close, he could see the scars across her cranium that balded her halfway back into her scalp. She might have been beautiful once. Even intelligent.

He picked up a dirt clod and threw it. It bounced off one slack hip, leaving a pink mark that he knew stung. She tossed her head and bounded after the others, away from the line of fire.

He looked up and saw the withered remains of a fruit tree straggling over him. That was why they didn't want to leave. He must have been interrupting a favored snack. He reached up and snagged one of the few fruits left. He didn't recognize it and it left a sticky residue on his hand after he tossed the fruit away.

The object rolled along the ground and disappeared in the tall grass even as he contemplated the frontal assault and the best way to join it.

A low hiss interrupted Jack's kamikaze tactics. *"Go away. I don't feel like playing now."*

A human voice, desperate. He recognized the central Dominion accent. Jack straightened. It seemed to be coming out of the ground. Cautiously he moved toward it, knowing that every good rat hole had a second entrance—and exit. Jack nudged a large grass divot in the same direction the fruit disappeared.

"Damn it, I don't want to play!" Grass and soft dirt fountained as the man came halfway out of the ground. He stopped, white hair in disarray, and stared at Jack.

Then, great tears began to stream down the man's pale face. "Oh, God," he said. "Oh, God. You've come back."

Jack palmed a grenade.

The man clambered weakly out of the hole. He held half a human skull in his hand. "I've been digging," he said. He dropped the ivory bone. "I've been digging in secret ever since the attack last year. I hoped—I knew you'd be back. As soon as I heard the ships come in, I knew. I bolted for my secret tunnel."

The man went to his knees in front of Jack. "Whoever you are, please, dear God, take me home!"

"Who th' hell are you?"

"I'm . . ." a stricken look came over the man's face and he gulped convulsively two or three times. "No, wait! I'm Mierdan. I'm a—I was a xenobiologist. I was captured twenty-three years ago. Please, either take me with you for the love of God, or kill me here!"

"Oh, shit." Jack stared down at the frail, wispy-haired man. Now he had to get off Klaktut alive. This man probably knew more about Thraks than any human being in existence. He reached down gently and helped Mierdan to his feet.

The ground exploded behind him as the Thraks came after them. They clambered up like visitors from hell.

Jack lobbed a grenade, picked the little man up by the waist and slung him over his shoulder like a sack of grain. He ran, accustomed to the strength of the armor, and feeling its lack. They were both panting when the Thraks caught up and fired.

The laser rifle in his hand made a dull *twang* sound. His hand went numb as the rifle spun away. Mierdan slipped from his left shoulder and hit the ground. He began to wail in despair.

Jack tore his ammo belt off and threw it at the wall of Thraks. They acted in reflex as he hoped they would: one of them shot at the belt of grenades. Even as its arms and weapon went up, Jack dove for the ground, drawing fire from the others.

There was a second, frozen in his mind: his body in midair and the blast from the Thraks' hand gun sending blue-orange fire from its muzzle.

When he landed, the grenades went off and he was deaf and dumb until Mierdan began to wiggle and complain underneath him.

His back felt wet and sticky. With a groan,

Jack rolled to his flank. Mierdan sat up, made a gagging sound and spewed bilious vomit over the grass. It scarcely showed among the litter of bodies.

Jack got up. He hurt. He'd been hit, but how badly he didn't know. Peppered with shard, if he were lucky. He swallowed hard. His chronos flashed an alarm at him. Thunder cut through the roar of warfare.

He had five minutes to make the transport. He took Mierdan by the arm and hauled him to his feet.

"C'mon," he husked. "It's now or never."

The little man didn't ask questions. They helped each other over the broken field and road to the flats where the Talons were waiting.

One man in ten came back.

But that one man came back triumphantly.

Jack handed Mierdan over to Staub and said, "This man has spent the last twenty years studying the Thraks."

They caught him swaying on his feet before he hit the deck.

Chapter 23

After the disinfecting, the blinding arc lights went away. Bogie's bedazzled sensors came back to a normal reading and he could see again. The hold stayed quiet. Across the deck, he could see a map etched on the wall. The language was symbolic and even he could understand that he could leave the ship by following the drawing. He moved away from his equipment rack and the crates marked STORM, J., and approached the schematic.

The sound of the cutting torches whined through the ship, and it shuddered. Bogie turned. His vessels and budding heart contracted and thudded wildly. He knew the sound from the shops he and Jack had visited.

When the bulkhead opened a second time, Bogie was ready. He launched upward from a crouch with a roar of synthetic noise, power-vaulted over the alien bodies, and ran to the escape hatches.

Two pods lay open, unused and functional. He dove into the nearest one, slammed the door shut and felt it begin to vibrate, made operational by the portal's closing. As it launched, he re-coiled into himself in shock, for he'd seen the

Ash-farel, and his soulmind could not comprehend the wrongness of the sight.

To have come so far, to no avail.

The Flexalinks could only curl so far, but the battle suit rolled as much into a ball as possible as the pod launched into hyperspace.

Left behind by the Ash-farel, losing FTL speed rapidly, the pod emerged somewhere in deep space.

"I thought," Mierdan said, chin propped on the edge of the medcrib, "that you'd lost that finger on account of me—but the doctor says that's an old injury. Anyway, the placental grafts are doing well and by the time we hit Mistwald, you'll be as good as new."

Jack rolled an eye at the scientist who'd scarcely stopped talking since Storm had awakened. He knew he was as good as new—he'd taken fire across his back, but his new skin only felt sunburned and he moved gingerly. He sat up in the crib. "What about you?"

Mierdan paused. He clamped his mouth shut. He was a spare, little man, with a sharp chin. He was working on growing a tuft of white beard at the point of it. He sighed. " I guess . . . I guess I'm going to be okay. I don't know." He wrapped his arms about his knees, hugging himself and looked across the hospital floor. "Until the truth comes out."

"The truth?"

Mierdan shook his head. "I lived when the others didn't. I—I stood by while the Thraks bred them and made . . fodder . . . out of them."

"Did you help? Could you have stopped it?"

"No! No, and no again."

Jack put his feet to the deck. It was cold. He shivered involuntarily, and his back pained him from the movement. "Then you did nothing wrong."

"But I worked for the Thraks."

"You survived." Jack stood up, and leaned on Mierdan's shoulder. "We've all done a bit of that. Do you know where I lost this finger and three toes?"

The xenobiologist shook his head.

"Then listen while I tell you. Keep pace with me while I walk the room."

Mierdan looked as if he'd bow under Jack's weight, but he didn't, other than to protest, "You shouldn't be up."

Jack answered, "I'm not staying up. But I heal faster when I'm up." And quietly, matter-of-factly, Storm told Mierdan as much of his story as he deemed wise.

Mierdan limped him back to the medcrib. His dark eyes were brimming as he lowered Jack down.

"Then you know," he said, "what I've been through."

"Some of it. A little more than the next man."

Mierdan buried his face in his hands. There was a noisy sob, and then the scientist forcibly buried it. He looked up. "They kept me alive," he said, "only because they thought I could help. I pretended to, and maybe I could have, but I didn't."

"Help what?"

"I know why the Thraks swarm."

Jack leaned back, pillowing his head on his good hand. The right one was still bruised from the shot that had torn the rifle away. "So do I. It's procreation, a mass hysteria procreation. And we've got some good indication that there's territorial rivalry with an ancient foe that drives them."

"There's more to it than that." Mierdan paused significantly. "Tricatada is the last, and only, fertile Thraks."

He broke the stunned silence. "Jack—are you all right? Do you have fever?"

Jack knocked the scientist's hand away as Mierdan sought to place it on Jack's forehead. "Are you telling me," he said, "that every *sand* planet has been populated by the one queen?"

"Yes. You can imagine how desperate they are. I've tried to explain to them that perhaps the overworking is contributing to the problem, but they're afraid she'll never produce a fertile egg. They swarm in hysteria, hoping above hope that one of the hatchers will be another queen, or even rarer, a king. When she goes, and she hasn't that long left to be producing, the Thraks begin to die off."

"Mierdan, are you certain?"

He shrugged and looked away again. "I've been her midwife for the last twenty years," he said.

Mierdan could have killed Tricatada and stopped the Thrakian League. Jack clamped his jaw shut tightly on what he wanted to say to that. The wiry man was not a murderer. Jack had no right to judge his actions.

But he did say, "We can stop *sand*."

"What?"

"You know what you know. We can use that knowledge to stop the Sand Wars."

Slender fingers tugged on the tuft of white hair. Mierdan shook his head. "She'll never agree. She can't. It—it's like stopping a birth in the middle of hard labor. It can't be done. The impetus demands that the birth happen. So her instincts drive her, and all the rest of the Thraks, and they cannot stop until a fertile egg is laid. Then she might be convinced to slow down a little."

"Do they have DNA?"

"No. At least, not that my crude instruments showed me."

Jack pointed a finger at him. "You'll think of something."

Mierdan's mouth dropped open. Then he shrugged. "Perhaps. Staub is pleased with me as I am. I can witness the true nature of the Thraks and the nature of the alliance Pepys has made." He stood up. "I've wearied you long enough. I'll be back later." He paused at the hospital portal. "And thank you."

Jack smiled. The little man hopped through the bulkhead and was gone. Jack lay back. The hope that Mierdan had given him made him want to reach out and grasp someone's hand tightly. It made the loneliness in him more palpable. He'd lost his armor. What was he without it? He felt more tired than he'd thought possible, turned his face toward the cool sheets and slept.

* * *

"—and don't tell St. Colin."

Colin heard the copilot's voice fade away abruptly as he approached the command post, and he came through the bulkhead with a wry smile. "Just what is it you don't want me to know?" He looked from Ivanoff the copilot to Jonathan, whose bulk nearly overwhelmed the area.

Jonathan frowned. "We've picked up a blip."

"Really? Ash-farel already?"

Jonathan paled visibly. "God in heaven. I hope not."

Colin was leaning over the instrument panels, searching the readouts eagerly. He stopped and turned back to his aide. "Good heavens, Jonathan, do stop that. That's why I've come all the way out here to this God-forsaken corner of space."

"What?" Dark-skinned Ivanoff paled as well. He rocked back in his command chair.

"I've come out to investigate what I can of them."

Jonathan sat down with a thud. "As near as I can tell, your eminence, they shoot first and communicate later."

"If that must be. It seems to have slipped everyone's mind that this is one of the first new alien races we've encountered in the last century. No one seems to want to find out what we're faced with."

Ivanoff muttered, "We're faced with coldblooded killers."

"So it seems, still—" Colin eyed the blip. Visible disappointment lowered his brows. "Whatever it is, it's too small for Ash-farel. I've heard their cruisers are immense."

Ivanoff came to attention. "That's an escape pod." He brought the image in sharper.

Colin looked at it oddly, then said, "I suppose we'd better fish it in."

They were all waiting in the docking area for the air lock to finish sealing the dock off. Jonathan put his beefy hand on Colin's shoulder.

"We don't know what's in there, your eminence. Perhaps you should retire to your cabin and I'll inform you."

Colin looked up. "Don't coddle me, Jonathan. I've seen more horrible sights than you can imagine. I don't intend to leave while they crack open that egg."

They watched together as two crewmen, dressed in environmental suits, approached the pod cautiously. It hissed as the portal door was wrenched open, and the two men just stared. One of them turned around and said, "It looks like a dead robot."

"What?" Colin came close to the window. The dock rotated so that he could get a look inside the pod. He shook off Jonathan's arm so that his aide couldn't feel him trembling. "Take it to my room," he said.

"Sir?"

"Take it to my room. And leave me alone." Colin pressed his lips together tightly and left the staging area.

It took four men to carry in the armor. Colin stood impassively, his hands tucked inside his many pocketed jumpsuit, and watched them. They were afraid to drop it, despite its weight. Jonathan hovered at the door.

"I don't want to be disturbed," Colin repeated. "See that I'm not."

His aide turned a puzzled look toward him. "I know that armor. . . ."

"Yes. I'm sure you do." Colin shut the door in his face. He walked to the Flexalink suit and bent over it for a moment. Emotion shook his hands so hard that he found it difficult to unscrew the helmet.

Escape pods were not found by accident in a quadrant of space where he expected open warfare. The deduction was obvious. Colin had been right about the area of the next attack. He'd only been wrong about when. This was Jack's armor, and it lay empty.

Empty of all but that other Jack both nurtured and feared.

Colin set the helmet aside and reached inward, touching the alien. It was both warm and featureless. It pulsated hesitantly under his hand.

"I'm a friend," the saint said, and waited.

Chapter 24

Amber woke in the night. She lay still for a moment, coiled in the warmth of pillow and blanket, and blinked, wondering what it was that woke her. She thought of Jack and the restlessness that plagued his nights. The thought made her smile. She was stretching out of her nest of blankets when the door opened abruptly and light stabbed her vision.

Sadie stood silhouetted in the frame. "There's been a complication," she said, "with your call to Jack."

"You've got an answer?"

"No. But there's been some unpleasantness—Green Shirts have been identified as raiders on Klaktut. Jack has been implicated as one of the ringleaders. I don't need to tell you the extent of the infiltration by the Thraks under the Alliance. We're in trouble if they decide to retaliate."

Amber got up, shivering. She pulled a blanket about her shoulders. "But the call went through?"

"Yes. Unfortunately, it attracted attention." Sadie moved aside, and another figure loomed in the doorway.

Vandover Baadluster shouldered the pawnbroker away. He smiled down at Amber. "An ancient adage," he murmured, "but true. 'You can run, but you can't hide.' " He snapped his fingers. The darkness at his back stirred, and she saw the two tall, insectoid sentries flanking him. He said, "Take her into custody. Pepys wants to talk to her."

"Sadie—"

The heavyset woman shrugged, her platinum curls mussed by the little sleep she'd had. "I can no longer help you, Amber. I'm sorry."

Vandover's smile spread. "I just love it when a plan comes together."

The Thraks moved forward, their faces in Kabuki masks of terror and intimidation. Amber stepped back, to the stand beside her bed, slender right hand going back for a weapon when the Thraks moved.

She'd heard Jack talk about fighting them, knew his hatred for them. But she'd not been prepared for their lightning, supple movements. There was no escape.

Baadluster put his hand upon her hair and caressed it as they dragged her past. The guards paused. He looked at Sadie. "A little visit to your cold lab. The emperor requests your cooperation."

If Sadie felt Amber's eyes upon her, she did not show it. The woman abandoned her bantering tone, and showed the cutting edge of her business side.

"Time is money, Vandover. If this is a social visit, I don't give tours through the cold vault."

Amber tensed, testing the hold of her captors.

Did Baadluster know about the Countess and what she had stored with her?

The Minister of War dropped his hand from Amber's hair. "This is not a visit, madame. I have a customer for you, someone I wish chilled down." He smiled at Amber, "You'll be less troublesome that way."

Jack worked with the film editors as soon as they returned to Mistwald to piece together the footage they were able to salvage. He sat with Staub and watched the rough frames.

"Will it stand up?" the commander said to him.

"I don't know. They're not going to want to believe us anyway—we need more footage."

"There isn't any more. We lost most of the equipment on Number One."

"I know," Jack answered. There was a moment of emptiness for himself but he shook it off. He turned his eyes away from the projection. "The Thraks have already branded us as butchers."

"Did you expect to be a hero?"

Jack took a pull on a lukewarm beer. He rolled it around his mouth as if it held an answer and swallowed. Finally, he said, "I've been around long enough to know we rarely get what we expect."

Staub raised gray-flecked auburn brows. "A cynic?"

He shook his head. "A realist."

A door opened. A moon-faced young man, the fresh recruit replacement for Chrysler who had died on Klaktut, leaned hesitantly in. "We have a visitor," he said. "Sir."

"Who is it?"

"One of the locals, sir. I'm told she's really important."

Jack got to his feet. Any Fisher fitting that description and visiting would almost have to be Mist-off-the-waters. He said, "Can I go with you, Staub?"

The recruit flushed. "Actually, sir, she's come to see you."

Worry prickled through Jack, and his recent healings felt the reaction. Staub stood. "I think we'd better both go. Where is she?"

"She wouldn't be closed in, sir, so we cleared the mess hall. . . ."

Jack was gone before the recruit finished.

She had her back to the door when he entered, but her round ears flicked and he knew she'd heard him come in. She stood with bowed shoulders, her tail in a despondent curve.

Her first words to him were: "Help me, Little Sun. The false emperor has taken Skal hostage."

"What? How?"

"He was summoned for a subspace call at the post in Fishburg. But when he got there, he found agents waiting for him. They . . ." The Fisher paused. Her large deep blue eyes filled with unshed tears.

"Is he alive?"

She nodded. A tear hung from one whisker, a diamond in the late afternoon light.

"You don't understand," Jack said to Mist as

gently as he could. "I've lost my armor. There's no way I can go in after him."

More tears brimmed in her eyes. "You will abandon him?"

"He's being held hostage, Mist. Shining furgrinning tooth will hold him until he's lost his value. It will take time to arrange things—"

"He does not have time!" Mist's anger hissed through her sharp Fisher teeth, and her ivory tail lashed the air. "You're a fool, Little Sun."

Her emotions pierced him. He had never felt so vulnerable, not even under Klaktut's bloody sun. "As much as I value Skal's friendship and yours, this is not my world. Your politics are not mine—"

"To *sand* with politics! He's being held because he's allowed this base to stay in operation. He's being held because of you! Shining furgrinning tooth is no fool. His spies have told him about the capabilities of the Green Shirts. Make no mistake—Skal is being held because of what you've done here, and if he's not ransomed within forty-eight hours, he will be sentenced to death without trial. We are barbarians here. If Skal dies, then Shining fur-grinning tooth will begin to round up innocents and condemn them, until we have no choice but to go to him and turn ourselves in."

Jack took a deep breath, figuring his options. With Bogie gone, he had few. "All right," he said. "I'll exchange myself for Skal."

Shock rippled across her otter face. "No!"

"A rescue will simply bring open warfare back. Do you want the fighting the way it was a few years ago? No, Shining fur-grinning tooth wants the rebel ringleaders he imagines and so we'll give him one. With luck he'll be so shocked to find it an off-worlder, he'll be unable to act. You get Skal as far away and out of sight as you can. Can it be done? I assume you have an underground?"

"Yes, there's still a Resistance."

"I see no other way."

Staub had been listening quietly but now he said, "You risk much."

Jack shrugged, saying, "What else can I do?"

Jack, who was so used to the simplicity of the Fisher life, found the imperial palace shocking. He had never been to Triata, even in the course of the civil wars he'd found himself in years ago, so he did not know what to expect. Mist piloted the skimmer over the city boundaries, and the clouds parted long enough to show him a city on stilts over a sapphire blue lake and river, Fishers going about their business by the thousands. No one looked up as the skimmer clouded their industry.

Mist showed her teeth. "How do you like our capital?" She seemed unconcerned, unworried how Triata compared to off-world cities he had visited. She piloted them along the river, where the stilted huts clustered in abundance. She pointed her sharp muzzle at the terraced hillside raising ahead of them, at the farthest end of the lake. Beyond, sharp, new mountains rose, their peaks tipped with blue snow. The palace reigned at the top of the terrace, its green marble splendor a sight that captured all attention, its columns and roofs carved into jade brilliant leaves and vines and tree trunks supporting lofty branches. It had been built around a courtyard. As they flew toward it, Jack could see the blue eyes of pools, fountain spray distorting their edges. The Green Shirt base could easily have fit inside the palace grounds. Not even the rose obsidite splendor of the Triad Throne could compare to this gem of Mistwald.

Birds from the lake strolled along the terrace grounds. There were modest little brown birds darting in and out of the reach of strolling majestic birds with fan tails the color of the rainbow. They reacted as the skimmer shadowed them, giving out trumpets of challenge. Jack saw clouds of insects hovering in place until he realized they were in nets, buoyed by the wings of their captives. As Fisher guards guided the skimmer into a parking barn, she wrinkled her muzzle at the insect clouds.

"Lunch," she said, and Jack realized the nets would be released, so the birds could feed.

She snapped at a guard anchoring the skimmer. "Tell Shining fur-grinning tooth I'm here. He's expecting me."

The guard did not ask her name. Jack watched him lope off, weapons belt rattling about his black slicker shorts. He jumped out of the skimmer and handed Mist down. The ivory Fisher looked deeply into his eyes.

"Thank you," she said, but he had the feeling she had settled for that after rejecting other choices.

He nodded gravely. "You're welcome."

Both of them knew she didn't mean for the help in dismounting. A phalanx of guards came trotting up before they'd left the parking barn. There was menace in their attitude, but they fell in behind Jack and Mist as she led him to the palace steps.

There were sixty steps of cool, green veined marble. At the top of them, sitting instead of standing, was a very battered Skal. He did not look pleased to see Jack.

His whiskers had been singed off one side of the muzzle. One eye was purpled and swollen. Mist sucked in her breath at his obvious mauling. He held a paw-hand close to his ribs. His breath whistled slightly.

For all that, he frowned at Jack. "So, my friend," he said, and his voice barely rose above a whisper. "You are my price."

Jack inclined his head. "The least I can do."

"Before you go in, I'll relay the message I received—it was intended for you."

"Me?"

"Yes. Amber sent to you from Malthen. She said, 'Tell Jack the mind-loop has been located and to come home.' "

Jack stood in stunned silence. His past—found. Amber had succeeded.

Skal licked split lips. "Any reply?"

"No. Not yet. Shining fur-grinning tooth can't hold me—I'll send an answer myself when you're safely out of here."

As they spoke, the phalanx of guards had spread

out and now ringed all three of them. Mist bent over Skal and helped him to his feet. The two Fishers started down the stairs until they met the wall of guards. Jack held his breath until the guards let them through.

He turned to the guard nearest him. "I believe the emperor is waiting." The Fisher dipped his muzzle, about faced and led the way.

The palace interior was as cool and dim as the inside of the rain forest, and looked little different, except that its fronds and branches were worked in stone and jade. The canopy overhead was entwined with vines and feathers—bird and insect wings. The light and cloud dappled sky of Mistwald could be seen through the opaque stonework.

The pad-pad of the guards' feet upon the marble was as loud as drums. Jack's boots overshadowed them. He saw the heavily muscled otter-man seated on a throne at the far end of the room.

"Well, well," Shining fur-grinning tooth called out happily. "I hope poor Skal knows the kingly ransom you've paid for his mange-eaten hide."

"You were expecting someone else?"

"No. Not unless you're not Jack Storm. Skal didn't know of course, I think he rather suspected the Elders were willing to make a martyr out of him. I think he'd have liked that. Now he has to slink away with the Resistance and lick his wounds."

Jack was allowed within a good-sized leap of the throne. Up close, he could see that Shining fur-grinning tooth was a russet and sable powerhouse of a Fisher—but that he had a certain unwholesomeness about him. Jack felt an instant dislike for the ruler of Mistwald.

Shining fur-grinning tooth showed his canines. "You do realize the base is exposed and cannot be allowed to continue."

"We gathered that." Jack checked his chronos computer. "By now, it's probably been evacuated. Anything left behind has been demolished. You won't get anything useful."

The otter-man's tail whipped out in agitation, but the being stilled himself with great difficulty. Then he grated out, "I have no more use for you, Jack Storm." He turned his head.

"Take him."

Before the shadowed interior behind the throne could boil with movement, a clear, high voice called out, "Jack! Run!"

Amber's words froze him as neatly in his tracks as a stunner. Armor materialized and two massive guards caught him up before he could free himself. Jack struggled until their gauntleted hands tightened harshly about his arms and he had no choice.

Amber, Vandover Baadluster, and Pepys stepped from behind the curtains. Pepys had chosen to wear his imperial red and gold robes. The greenish cast of the Triata palace did not illuminate his pasty skin well. Baadluster looked as sepulchral as usual within the black robes he affected for his office.

And as for Amber, she wore the dark blue she loved, in a dress she would never have chosen for herself, too close about her hips and neckline and dipping low between her breasts. But she was beautiful even now, with her hair about her like a tawny cloud of indignation. Even as he watched, she twisted a hand free, went for a knife in her boot heel, and came up, knife cocked at Baadluster's throat while Pepys shouted, "Halt!"

Vandover backhanded her and it took both suits of armor to wrestle Jack to the ground. They knelt upon his back as he lay breathing hard and Baadluster was more gentle when he took the knife from Amber's hand. She placed the back of the other one against her face as if to cool the wound.

Pepys looked at the Fisher emperor. "Leave us," he said.

The being gave him a look of hatred, got down from his throne, signaled his guards, and left the palace hall.

Pepys gathered up his robes and sat down on the dais edge with a sigh. "You're mine," he said. "I can do anything I want to with you now."

"Then do it," Jack said. His chin ground into the marble floor and his back where the Knights rested hurt like hell, but he was done with running. "Do whatever it was you came for. But before you do, I want you to know we got what we went for on Klaktut. We have proof that you've made a treaty with monsters—not once, but twice."

Baadluster spoke, his voice a well-oiled machine. "I always said it would only take one honest man to turn the Shirts around. And you, your majesty, drove them together."

Pepys waved a weary hand. "If you promise good behavior, Storm. I'll have them let you up."

Jack twisted his neck to look at the emperor. "If I get up, you'll have to kill me here, because I'm damned if you're going to drag me anywhere to make an example out of me."

"And that's your promise?"

Jack glared.

With a sigh, Pepys signaled and added, "Just hear me out."

Amber went to Jack with a half-sob and helped him up. She smoothed his hair back from his face and touched his back gently, as if knowing the scars he bore there. Jack took her into the cradle of his arm. He looked at Pepys.

"You're a traitor, Pepys, and I now have proof—"

The emperor cut him short. "I know, Storm. I know. We're both traitors, and that is not important now." His cat-green eyes glittered at them. "You're both free to go if you will help me in one matter. Agreed?"

Amber said bitterly, "Where do we leave our souls?"

"No catch, my lady. No catch at all, because I am a desperate man. I killed and lied and cheated to get my throne, and I do it to keep it, but in between, I work very hard to keep a number of humans alive and thriving. So my petty grievances with you two must be put aside for the—" Pepys grimaced. "The so-called greater good. You have to help me, Jack. That is why I've come to Mistwald, why I've come to you instead of having you brought back to Malthen. So that you could see how desperate I am."

Amber started to say something else, but Jack stopped her. Pepys was serious. "What is it?"

"It is a matter that could set off a war that will make our grievances with the Thraks seem trivial. Even the Ash-farel pale beside it—human against human, with no respite but total annihilation of our race."

"What?" Amber asked, confused, but Jack felt a chill in his bones.

Pepys rubbed a weary hand over his face. "St. Colin has disappeared. He went out to investigate the Ash-farel. He met up with an empty suit of armor and took it. Where he went, no one knows. But the Walkers and others won't leave any stone unturned until he is found. No accusation unsaid. No kingdom unchallenged."

"Tell me about the suit of armor."

The emperor looked him in the eyes. "Jonathan was hysterical, but he said it was your armor."

Amber's hand grasped Jack's arm tightly, but she said nothing.

Jack eyed Pepys a moment longer. "I'll go," he said finally. "If you'll give me your resignation when I return."

The fine red hair of the emperor drifted about his face, but it could not obscure his expression. It was one of defeat. Pepys inclined his head. "So be it," he said. "The throne is yours, if there is one left."

Jack pulled himself up straight. He did not

want or need a throne. But now, at last, what he had sworn to accomplish was within his grasp. With one last quest, he could finally see the end of the Sand Wars and avenge the betrayal of his people!

DAW

C.J. CHERRYH
THE ALLIANCE-UNION UNIVERSE

The Company Wars
- ☐ DOWNBELOW STATION   (UE2227—$3.95)

The Era of Rapprochement
- ☐ SERPENT'S REACH   (UE2088—$3.50)
- ☐ FORTY THOUSAND IN GEHENNA   (UE1952—$3.50)
- ☐ MERCHANTER'S LUCK   (UE2139—$3.50)

The Chanur Novels
- ☐ THE PRIDE OF CHANUR   (UE2292—$3.95)
- ☐ CHANUR'S VENTURE   (UE2293—$3.95)
- ☐ THE KIF STRIKE BACK   (UE2184—$3.50)
- ☐ CHANUR'S HOMECOMING   (UE2177—$3.95)

The Mri Wars
- ☐ THE FADED SUN: KESRITH   (UE1960—$3.50)
- ☐ THE FADED SUN: SHON'JIR   (UE1889—$2.95)
- ☐ THE FADED SUN: KUTATH   (UE2133—$2.95)

Merovingen Nights (Mri Wars Period)
- ☐ ANGEL WITH THE SWORD   (UE2143—$3.50)

Merovingen Nights—Anthologies
- ☐ FESTIVAL MOON (#1)   (UE2192—$3.50)
- ☐ FEVER SEASON (#2)   (UE2224—$3.50)
- ☐ TROUBLED WATERS (#3)   (UE2271—$3.50)
- ☐ SMUGGLER'S GOLD (#4)   (UE2299—$3.50)

The Age of Exploration
- ☐ CUCKOO'S EGG   (UE2371—$4.50)
- ☐ VOYAGER IN NIGHT   (UE2107—$2.95)
- ☐ PORT ETERNITY   (UE2206—$2.95)

The Hanan Rebellion
- ☐ BROTHERS OF EARTH   (UE2209—$3.95)
- ☐ HUNTER OF WORLDS   (UE2217—$2.95)